ZODIAC PRISON

BOOK 3

R.C. LUNA

OTHER WORK BY R.C. LUNA

Welcome to book three of the Warrior Shifter series. If you enjoy this series it would mean the WORLD to me if you left a review so other readers can learn about my work. Subscribe to my newsletter and unlock **The Zodiac Codex** – your exclusive guide to character sheets, folklore, behind-the-scenes insights, and an exploration of the Zodiac natal chart that shapes the Warrior Shifter world.

The *Warrior Shifter* series
Zodiac Shadows (prequel)
Zodiac Fate (Book 1)
Zodiac Chaos (Book 2)
Zodiac Prison (Book 3)
Zodiac Throne (Book 4)

This book is dedicated to the beautiful island of Puerto Rico. Thank you for inspiring me through your magic.
"La isla del encanto"

CONTENTS

LETTER FROM THE AUTHOR

Welcome to the third book in the Warrior Shifter series. This is a dark fantasy romance, a work of fiction that delues into intense storylines and themes that could be sensitive to some readers. This book contains a range of trippers, including steamy, open-door romance, betrayal, despair, explicit sexual conduct, and violence – physical, mental, and psychological. Please take this warning seriously and proceed with care.

You may find yourself walking through hell alongside these characters, feeling their pain, their passion, and their struggles. But on the other side, there is strength – perhaps even your own, reflected back at you.

To reach that strength, you must endure the journey.Please read responsibly.

-R.C. Luna

CHAPTER 1

"**D**arkness within darkness. Gateway to all understanding." - Lao Tzu

I remembered this passage that was etched into the marble stone in our Magical Sciences class as Zayne, my nagual combat instructor and mentor, and I trekked in our jaguar forms through the dark jungle of the Gemini House. All manner of jungle creatures lived here in the thick, damp landscape. I was always surprised at the various species in the Zodiac territories. Variants of the familiar spiders and snakes, worms and gorillas. Yet there were so many more, some as small as the cueyatl, a tiny frog with a tongue so poisonous it could corrode your body with a single swipe. Or the ahuizotl, a dog-like creature with hands instead of paws and a hand on its tail with sharp claws. These creatures could also see perfectly under the cover of night. It made it nearly impossible for anyone to live in this precarious habitat. This is where the hunters became the hunted.

The clouds covered the moon, and it would have been pitch black if it wasn't for our night vision. My jaguar form was as black as the night and adept at seeing in the dark, equipped with eyes that amplified even the slightest light peeking through the faintest parts of the clouds above. I wondered what understanding I was supposed to have right now as I lived the words of the timeless quote.

Up ahead, that's it. Unable to communicate with Zayne in my nagual form, I thought this to myself as I peered through the bush at the creature crouched on the side of the riverbank. We blended with the dark energy of the night and watched her in utter silence, undetectable by Fae senses in our jaguar forms. It was a cihuatl. Thick, long strands of black-and-grey hair flowed from the top of her head. At her back were two dark-grey, slimy, scaled bat-like wings, and her belly was swollen from pregnancy. Because of her crouched position, her legs were hidden from view. Her face looked like it had no flesh, just the skull, because of the thin, transparent skin and veins that covered it. These were the creatures of nightmares. They brought sickness to Fae villages, hunted the children that fell ill, then stole them from their families. They drew power from the pain and suffering of the surviving family members. The creatures were nearly seven feet tall, rare and hard to find, mainly because of how they reproduced.

At the moment, with her eagle-like claws, she was tearing into what appeared to be young human flesh. My hackles rose as we crept toward her, my claws digging into the ground with every step. As we got closer, I glanced over at Zayne, who gave me a short nod. We emerged from the cover of the jungle, ready to attack.

The moment he lurched toward her, I rushed to the creature's side and locked my teeth over her wings. I anticipated that she would immediately try to fly away rather than fight. Just as I did, Zayne went for the neck. The cihuatl easily flung him aside with one swipe of her arm. It was strong, and Zayne was stunned from the blow. The creature turned, trying to throw me off its back, and I dug my teeth even harder into those slimy wings. It tried to grab at me, but I dug my back legs into the ground as I locked my jaws on the wing's bones and heard a few snaps. It grasped me with its clawed hand and tried to inject me with the venom she carried in her blood. But it was no use; her claws couldn't penetrate my jaguar's flesh. This was what made us so unique and so powerful as protectors of Zol Stria.

The cihuatl wrapped her arm around me and yanked me off of her, flinging me with the force of a semi-truck. I landed with a loud thump against a jagged boulder. A moment later she began to bat her wings in an effort to escape. I lunged after her again, and she swiftly avoided my grasp and maneuvered herself behind me. Before I could react, I felt her sharp talons dig into my back as she lifted me into the air with her. Her strong, powerful wings flapped, the wounds from my attack wearing on her, but she pushed hard. My heart raced in a fit of panic when we rose off the ground. She could drop me anywhere and make her escape. We had been searching for her for three months, and I wasn't going to let her get away. We needed her.

I thrashed in a fit of rage and her talons gave way just a little. I couldn't reach her with my mouth or my claws, and I couldn't use my elemental powers in this form.

This mission is fucked.

Just as I thought this, she dipped lower to the ground, slamming me against the earth before lifting off again. My mind raced. *Should I shift back to human form?* The second I did, my skin would be filled with lethal diseases at the mere touch of one of her claws. But just then something crashed into her, and she began to tumble back down. It was Zayne. He'd leapt from the ground onto her back! I felt his weight send us hurtling down. Just as she began to fall, she released me, and my four legs landed firmly on the jungle floor. I ran out of the way as Zayne and the cihuatl plunged to the ground where I had been standing a heartbeat earlier. Instantly I was on her back, her wing once again in my mouth. As I tore into her left wing, the bitter-tasting blood spilled into my mouth.

The Zol Beast Keeper at the Academy had taught us that if anyone even touched cihuatl blood, their bodies would rapidly deteriorate with a cancerous plague. The only thing happening to me right now was my gag reflex; it was triggered by the god-awful taste. Once again, I was grateful for the gift of being a nagual and immune to Fae venom.

Zayne landed his canines into her neck, and a high-pitched scream left her throat. The creature that had just been towering over us stumbled to the ground with a thud, and Zayne landed on top of her. Once a nagual had you in their deadly jaw-lock, there was little, if anything, you could do to break free. Right now, she was struggling to breathe because his grip almost pierced into her veins through her hard scales. But he wouldn't kill her, at least not if he could help it. We needed information.

She thrashed about and kicked out her bony ostrich legs in protest. I padded closer, and she turned her cold, emotionless, reptilian eyes toward mine. She seemed to be trying to shoot venom from her throat at me, but it was no use under Zayne's tight grip. She would lose her breath soon if she didn't simply give in. She was finally realizing that she was outmatched, because she let out an unearthly squeal for breath. Zayne held on a few seconds longer, and when her eyes bulged, he released her.

She reached a clawed limb up to her throat and began to cough. Now that she was down, I shifted into my human form and stood there, completely naked save for the long, black, wavy hair that fell down my back. I called the dark to my fingertips and brought fire to my palms. The creature squirmed in pain on the ground as I raised a Zol rune around us. It was a circle of my fire element, forming the zodiac symbols to channel their power and serve as a conduit of the magic we needed to complete the mission. It was incredible how far I'd come. Two years ago I could barely channel fire in just one direction, now I was creating fire runes. Zayne remained a breath away from the cihuatl, ready to leap at her in a single heartbeat.

I chanted the incantation, "*Etchi nal Xila.*" *Darkness within darkness. Show me so I may understand.*

As soon as I finished, the blaze of the Zol rune began to glow even brighter, threatening to singe my back and legs with the heat. But I didn't move an inch as sweat began to form on my brow. My human form, or "Zol skin" as they taught us to say at the Academy, had a very high tolerance for heat because of my elemental power, but even still, if it consumed me, I would still burn, only slower.

The cihuatl looked around, winded, and just as she placed her clawed hands on the bloodstained ground to push her pregnant body upward to stand, Zayne took one step toward her and tore her abdomen open with his fangs. An ear-piercing shriek left her throat as her insides were exposed and spilled out all over the ground. It was critically important to our mission that the fetus was extracted while she was still alive.

I reduced the heat level of the fire rune and looked out past it, feeling the eyes of the jungle upon us. Her death released her dark energy. All of the torment, fear and agony this monster had caused and collected within her soul spilled out of her. An inky black mist filled the air within the fire circle. This was our bonus. I eagerly drew it toward me, soaking it up hungrily. A monster this deeply evil expelled an enormous amount of darkness that I used to replenish my own powers. I bared my teeth at Zayne, instinctively protective of my bounty, as he also pulled it in. But I didn't need to challenge him. There was plenty to go around.

"Sick. That must be it..." I said to Zayne as he got busy studying the creature.

Without lifting his gaze in my direction, he gave me a single nod of acknowledgment and continued to sniff and study the glowing, decomposing blue fetus that was still alive on the jungle floor. The cihuatl was a terrible sight, and her insides smelled of rotten flesh. They reproduced by stealing the fetus out of the belly of any warm-blooded creature, Fae or beast. They swallowed it whole, turning the creature into one of them while inside the womb, slowly infecting it with all of the diseases they carried. That's why these creatures didn't resemble each other. They turned into a hybrid of the life they stole and their beastly genes.

Over the years, the mages had created wards of protection over pregnant women that hid their unborn children from the senses of the cihuatl. This had made it very difficult for these creatures to reproduce and had reduced their numbers to near extinction. However, they would never become extinct. There were always those unfortunate mothers who had trouble getting the wards. Mothers who couldn't afford the wards included those outcasted from Zol society for anything ranging from mating with humans to various other forms of transgression, and, of course, there were those who would use the cihuatl as revenge or punishment on a new mother.

In an instant, I felt my face flush with embarrassment. I realized that this was my first time being naked in front of Zayne. I quickly shifted back to a nagual. Shapeshifter. Creature of demons and darkness. The trouble now was that we couldn't communicate with words in our nagual form. Only mated nagual could do that. So he went on sniffing at the rotted insides of the cihuatl. Then he picked up the glowing, acrid blue fetus with his teeth. I nearly threw up at the thought of the horrific tastes that must be filling his mouth. He lifted his gaze from the carnage and met my curious stare, bolting out of there heartbeats later with me keeping pace with him.

Our mission was complete, and now we would have some answers.

CHAPTER 2

As soon as we arrived at the Aries Academy campus, we ran directly to the ceremonial atrium behind the greenhouse. Zayne dropped the decaying body, which was still moving and taking its last breaths, on the ground in the middle of the summoning circle. Two Master Zol Sen, never seen unless at a ritual like this, were waiting for us in their long white robes with golden embroidery, along with the dean of Advanced Incantations and other academic instructors.

The world of the Zol Stria is incredibly complex and every day I learn something new about how all our lives are influenced by the cosmos and our surrounding universe. Zol Stria exists in tandem with the mortal realm, Earth. The world of Zol Stria is hidden behind twelve gates and is the soul of the planet, which is governed by the zodiac. The twelve constellations, visible on earth as the sun passes through each one, define our very existence. The position of Earth in relationship to the sun and the stars at the moment of birth for any creature on our planet outlines their soul's journey during this lifetime and defines the soul contracts they signed before taking their first breath. The Zol's journey, is the soul's journey. The struggles one has, the milestones they will experience and the lessons they must learn in order to continue to evolve and grow is mapped out for them. ***The stars write the path.*** This is the mantra of all of the people of Zol Stria.

Here, Zol means soul. It is the deity that is within you. The creatures of Zol Stria are able to channel and harness the power of the constellations, in an effort to maintain balance between our realms and in harmony with the universe. The idea that the Zol is holy and above all things became clearer to me the more I lived among the people of Zol Stria and I have now taken it on as my belief, too.

Zayne and I shifted back into our human forms. One of the apprentices approached me, and I gave her a grateful nod as she slipped a loose cotton wrap dress on me while Zayne pulled on jeans and a T-shirt. We were both in need of a good shower, but we would stay on and watch the ceremony unfold.

"Glad you made it back without decomposing from disease first," Jenna, my brown-skinned, jade-eyed nagual bestie, whispered to me as I went to stand next to her.

I reached both my hands to my throat and pretended to choke myself, sticking my tongue out and rolling my eyes. Then she nudged me, and I nudged her back playfully. We were in our third year at the Academy. Trent still held my heart, but our long-distance romance was wearing on me. We saw each other whenever we could, every few months or so. I figured out that if I snuck through the less-protected Sagittarius Gate, no one would notice. But it was such a long trip, and it was forbidden to cross the Gates without orders, so I was taking a huge risk.

Trent was growing in rank and had become a top mafia boss. By some miracle, he'd won back the trust of Solana, the most notorious leader of the Dark Zodiac on the other side of the Gates. The last time I'd visited, Trent wouldn't say much about her, which bothered me because I counted on him to give me intel. Our unit believed she still had at least one of the two missing relics, if not both. We had to get those relics back; they gave her way too much power. With Trent being immortal and me having hundreds of years of life ahead of me, we agreed to spend time apart, giving us valuable time for him to earn her trust enough to get the relics back while I continued building my skills in the Academy.

But it didn't matter how logical our plan sounded; Solana was a ruthless bitch who deserved to be destroyed for all the pain she had caused me. But every time I brought this up to him, he tried to convince me to see past my thirst for revenge to the bigger picture.

He would explain how her operation was too big for me to go at her guns blazing. We needed a strategy, and to form a strategy we needed intel, but it was hard to come by. Especially with Trent suddenly becoming tight-lipped. I did know that her focus was currently on Europe and the Middle East, and she had left Trent to oversee the North and South Americas operation. He made it seem like there was a lot she still hid from him.

I thought she would crucify him when he told her that the naguals had retrieved the Blood Ruby in our last mission. But she didn't. She was livid, of course, but when she found out Ixia had the Stone Mind and that the nagual were sent in to retrieve both, she considered it more of a casualty than a fuck up on his part. When he explained that he was using the Blood Ruby to take down the Miami Mafia, who was being led by Ixia, she didn't kill him. Instead, she reprimanded him, had him locked in a lead cell without blood for a while, then released him back into her ranks.

But I wondered what he wasn't telling me. I wondered why she would forgive him so easily when the relics were key to bringing back the UnZol King, who happened to be her great uncle, and creating the world she desired. I suspected there was much more to his relationship with her, and the more I thought about it, the more upset I became.

The night was cool while the air was supercharged with magical kinetic energy. Jenna and I and the rest of our unit—Bjorn, Lex, Andres, Eliana and Axel—were all present at the ceremony. These were the other nagual who'd made it across the Gates with me for our transformation into jaguar shifters, and now, after three years together at the Academy, they had become my family. About thirty more students filed around in the Zodiac rune, as there hadn't been a sacrifice of a cihuatl's still-living fetus for hundreds of years. This was more exciting than a solar eclipse on the summer solstice.

"What is that thing? It smells," Jenna asked, her long, golden-brown curls swishing across her back as she shook her head and crinkled her nose from the stench.

"You mean what *was* that thing," I corrected her. "I think the child was dragon-Fae. See the wings?"

"A baby dragon!" Jenna growled.

"Converting the babies of other Fae is what they do. It's one of the reasons they're so depraved," I whispered, shaking my head.

The masters of ceremony were at their places. The wind rustled through my dress as it blew, bringing with it the powerful energy of the cosmos summoned by the Zol Sen. This ancient wind swept toward the now-still carcass in front of us. Light sparkled all around and ignited the dark, as their hands brought forth a surge of energy toward the center of the Zodiac wheel where the fetus lay. From the floor the unborn child lit on fire and an image was clearly seen amidst the flames that it produced. Darkness within darkness. For over a year our team had been searching for any information that would lead us to the Blade Bone and the Devil's Eye, the two missing relics of the Unzol King.

Maybe today we would get answers.

And from the smoke and wind, grew the flame that brightened the air and within it was much more than visions of the Blade Bone or the Devil's Eye. No, those were not there in the flames. What I saw before me made my skin crawl and my eyes widen. My mouth began to gape open, and I clamped it shut. For the first time since I came to know the world of the Fae, I could not believe my eyes.

Instead of seeing what each of us was searching for, what we saw was me. I was standing there within the flames in a long, black gossamer flowing dress. The vision continued to show me climbing a large staircase to the top of a

Mayan pyramid. My dress was so long it cascaded several feet down the steps as though it was wind materialized, flowing obediently behind me as I walked. At the top of the steps was a man. Scratch that, he was a king. And when he held out his hand, I reached for him. I joined him on the top of the pyramid. We faced each other, then turned, coldly looking over the top of the pyramid at the countless Fae that spread out in immeasurable numbers in front of us.

"That's you," Jenna nudged me as I gaped at the vision.

"But how?" I winced. I had no idea what was happening right now.

"That man. The one I'm standing with. Is that?" I wondered out loud.

"That's the Unzol King. You wear his relics. The Blood Ruby, see you have the ring. The Stone Mind, the knife is at your side. The Blade Bone, the sword is strapped to your back. The Devil's Eye is that necklace you have on. And the Snake Tongue, the Sabre, it's sitting there next to the Heart." Her voice broke ever so slightly as she released a ragged breath. This did not look good. In fact, it looked like I was with the most evil and wicked Fae to have ever existed.

This made me look like a traitor. Like I was the enemy and even though I clearly wasn't the enemy now, I would be soon. I felt harsh stares being thrown in my direction. I had a deflector spell up, as I always did around other Fae. And yet I could feel them trying to penetrate it and draw out my thoughts and emotions in this very moment. I looked around, uncertain as to what to do. Jenna didn't budge. She stood protectively at my side, and the rest of my nagual unit, sensing the tension begin to rise, formed a protective crescent around me. Each one of them were in the defensive positions we had learned in combat training. They were prepared to fight for me. My jaguar stirred within me; she felt extra powerful after soaking in the cihuatl's dark energy. Yet still, there were very powerful professors and Zol Sen all around us. I didn't want to fight anyone. I was completely confused, but in all of this confusion, I was grateful for the protection of my team.

The light of the vision dwindled out and disappeared. It left them all there, staring at me.

"I have no idea what that's about," I said, keeping my tone calm and steady.

Zayne spoke next. "Everyone, relax. She's not the enemy."

A Master Zol Sen stepped forward to say something, which was highly unusual because their kind rarely spoke. "The prophecy is written."

Everyone in the atrium hushed in silence as they strained their ears to listen. Then, as one, the two Master Zol Sen said together, louder, "The prophecy is written."

I maintained a cool look on my face even though my eyes wanted to bulge out of their sockets. "What does he mean, 'the prophecy is written?'" I said in a low voice out of the side of my mouth to Zayne.

It means...run. Zayne said this to me not with his words, but with a swipe of his finger along his arm. It was a kind of sign language passed down from nagual to nagual. This way we could communicate with each other without anyone else knowing what we were saying.

Even though I understood his hand gesture, I was still so shocked from seeing the vision that it took me several heartbeats to realize what was happening. I watched Zayne's jeans and T-shirt shred to pieces as his bristly dark jaguar took over. In moments he embodied the feral black beast of his Fae form, and so did the other six nagual. But I remained locked in my human form, still processing what I had just seen and what I was feeling all around me. In an instant, I had become everyone's enemy. I couldn't stay frozen, because if I did the powerful magic of the Fae in attendance would quickly overpower my own. I took three measured steps back just as the Professor Mantua shot a web of lightning around me. She also cast an incantation designed to keep me from transforming and locking me in my current form. But she was one second too late, and I had already shifted.

The moment I was back in my jaguar form I walked through the lightning net, and it stung, but thanks to the absorption of the cihuatl's dark energy, the impact on me was minimal.

I ran as fast as I could into the surrounding Sacred Forest without stopping. My legs grew heavy from the pounding, and my heart raced in my chest. I still didn't know what I was running from, but there I was. Doing it. I looked left and right and saw my unit running next to me. We had an escape route that we had devised some time ago. We had set up a heavily warded location where we would meet in the event of emergencies like this. It was at the edge of the forest, a part of the woods long forgotten by everyone. If anything ever happened to any of us, we all knew to go there.

We scattered and spread out among the tall pines that surrounded the campus, purposely covering a lot of ground by running into rivers and entering caves. Our training included many nights sleeping under the stars in this forest; it was our territory, and even the Zol Wolves steered clear. Within the hour, and after an extra twenty miles of terrain covered between us all to mask our trails, we all had arrived at our safe house. The low branches of the surrounding trees hid the cabin built into the side of a mountain. As soon as we arrived, we split up and searched the property to make sure no one had followed us, then we transformed back into our human forms.

We opened the heavy wooden door, and the smell of stale wood and forest mildew wafted over me. The gas lamps on the walls sprang to life with the use of my fire element, the light casting over the simple tan couch with its beige-and-teal pillows. A soft teal rug covered the floor, and a large, beige wicker lamp hung over a dark-brown dining table. Jenna and I had fun decorating the place little by little. Our ideas were boho-chic but not too feminine so the guys would feel good about hanging out here too. My eyes darted over to the big brown bean bag in the corner with a beige blanket draped over it.

That's the spot where I went to cry. I had shed many tears on that bean bag, thinking about Trent and debating our decision to have a long-distance relationship. I had stopped stalking him with the Wall of Mirrors after I had seen him once at a dinner with Solana. I knew they would be doing things like that, but I hated seeing it. And sometimes I couldn't even see him, making me wonder if he had his own counter spell for the mirrors. Never mind the fact that it was a complete violation of his trust to spy on him like that.

"What is up with that vision?" Lex demanded as he stared down at me, concern lacing his expression along with anger and confusion.

After all our training, I trusted this unit with my life. Together, as a team, we would sort this all out. I shook my head in disbelief as I reached for the clothing we had stashed in our cabin. The soft white T-shirt and camouflage sweatpants I yanked on were a small comfort after the run.

"Your guess is as good as mine," I said.

CHAPTER 3

W e immediately got to work joining our magic together to cast a deflector spell over the cabin. No one would ever find this place. During my second year at the Academy, when we had first discovered this old cabin, Damian had placed a concealment spell over it. Anyone looking would only see a reflection of the area around it and not the actual building. We couldn't be seen, but we could be sensed. However, with our reinforced deflector spell in place, it would be impossible to detect our presence within the walls.

We met here every new moon to study together, discuss our challenges and setbacks and work on our issues. And to take Zol Dust shots after finals, of course. Zol Dust was a vodka-like drink laced with star dust, or so they said. All I knew was it was really hard to come by and I couldn't do more than one shot before getting lit. Besides, after I came down off the Zol Dust, I would start to think of Trent and our long-distance relationship. I felt kind of miserable about it most of the time.

"This doesn't look good for you," Jenna said as she went to the fridge to pour herself a glass of water. Her eyebrows knitted. After all the battles she and I had faced over the semester, she was more like family than a friend.

"I know, amiga. And I don't know what to do." I began to pace. "What did the Zol Sen mean by 'the prophecy is written?'"

"The cihuatl are never wrong," Zayne said gravely. He sat down at the dining table, his hand sweeping through his soft golden hair. The cihuatl, who lived only on the suffering of others, were dark windows to answers. Through the prayers and chants of the Zol Sen, the burning of a corrupted cihuatl fetus, while still alive, would illuminate a great truth being withheld. A truth that would lead to the destruction of those casting the incantation. After today's ritual, it would be the belief of all the Zol Sen that I was a conspirator of their destruction.

"In that vision, it appeared as though you were mated to the UnZol King," Zayne said plainly, his face cold and unyielding.

Looking around the room, I could see the same expression on the others. But I wasn't fazed by the feral rage I could sense thrumming through the room. I knew with every part of my dark, shadow-spun soul that we were all upset over the same thing. We were seven powerful proteges, led by the fierce but honorable Master Nagual Zayne. And we had sworn to keep each other safe.

"The Council has been desperate to track down the missing relics. Pluto will be returning for the first time in two hundred years. There is an urgency to retrieve all the relics before then, for fear the return of Pluto will open a portal to the UnZol King. It is believed that the Dark Fae currently have two of the missing relics. It's a long shot, but the Council believes the Dark Fae will try anything to get their hands on the other four and bring him back. Now you're showing up in the cihuatl vison at the top of a pyramid, mated to the UnZol King. You've just become enemy number one. The single most wanted outlaw in all of Zol Stria." Zayne's voice was almost too soft. Too controlled. It was too accepting of that fate.

"What if they're wrong? You said the visions have never been wrong, but then again, how many times has it been done? And could the vision have been manipulated somehow? Maybe it was planted there by the Dark Fae? Perhaps someone seeking revenge on me? Like Ixia or Solana? They are still both at large and out to get me." I shook my head, attempting to clear away the confusion but knowing it was pointless.

Lex came over and draped an arm around my shoulder. Bjorn wouldn't break from his position by the door, listening to our conversation from across the room. It comforted me to see him standing there, knowing the greatest warrior of Aries Academy was standing watch. He had earned his place as the Elite Zol Warrior, undefeated in the Academy, breaking records in sword fighting, combat training and martial arts. He had been hand-picked by the Vicars of Aries House to protect the heirs and become the House Nightslayer upon graduation, which was an honor bestowed to only a select few nagual over the centuries.

I looked over to the kitchen where Andres had taken out a few glasses and was pouring liquor into them. To my relief, he wasn't adding any Zol Dust. I certainly wasn't up for that.

"We all need to relax," Andres said with a slight, light-hearted smile. His comment was a welcome distraction from the seriousness of the conversation. The light from the gas lamps cast shadows on his thick black hair that swept over his eyes and accentuated his strong jawline.

I walked right over, picked up one of the glasses, and downed the bitter drink fast. Eliana came up next and stood just in front of Andres, her body making contact with his, and she took her shot too. The rest of our unit followed.

"The vision can't be wrong. There is no magic powerful enough to 'override' the image we saw. Plus, there are so many wards and security protocols in place around a ritual as significant as the cihuatl sacrifice that there is no way it could have been influenced," Zayne explained.

Axel spoke next, his Texan accent serving as a momentary distraction from the seriousness of his words. "They're upset as all get out, but I just don't understand why. It's just Sash. What if this UnZol King doesn't want to be bothered? I mean, what makes him so freaking special?"

"The prophecy," Zayne said. "The Dark Zodiac rebels we have managed to question say that a prophecy was written in the ancient scrolls, burned during the Faellen Wars, that he would return at the hands of Pluto. You know, Pluto being the other name for the god of the Underworld, also known as Hades in Greek mythology. They say that at the return of the planet Pluto to Earth so shall the Severed King rise and deliver his people to freedom. And because his body was severed into six pieces, well, it makes sense that it would be him. The old scroll isn't public information; I only know about it from my time working with the Council in the ancient archives. They joked about it. You know, things like, 'Whose side will you be on when Pluto returns.'" He cocked his head to one side, directing his gaze to me. "And if I remember correctly, there's something about him needing a mate to be able to complete his return because our mates are our anchors in this world." Zayne's cold eyes remained locked on mine. His wife was his Zol Mate, and she was killed in the Faellen Wars along with his two children.

"So, let's say the vision is right. That Sasha is destined to mate with the UnZol King. What will the Council do?" Axel asked.

"If this is what the Council believes, then they are already looking for her. Every creature under the stars will be hunting for Sasha. There will be a bounty on her head until she is returned to them. It would be my guess that if she were to be caught, they'd lock her up so that the UnZol King won't be able to access her to fulfill the prophecy we all saw. Or..." Zayne hesitated. "They may have her killed." He paced the room, his jaw clenched, and his handsome features concentrated on the floor in front of him.

"In that case, what are we going to do about it?" Jenna asked, her brows furrowed as she glared at Zayne, folding her arms in front of her.

I rubbed my sweaty palms against the cotton of my pants as I paced the room. My head began to pound as I considered all the angles. "Well then, I think we only have one option. I have to turn myself in. This way no one gets hurt, and I don't bring that prophecy to light."

Zayne shook his head. Bjorn, previously leaning against the wall as he guarded the entrance, stood upright and also shook his head. Within a few seconds everyone was looking at each other while I was still pacing, wringing my hands together.

"You can't turn yourself in, Sasha," Jenna said. "You know as well as I do, this will quickly turn political. The Houses will use your entrapment as their own victory to gain favor from the masses. And because you are an Aries, the Aries House will use it to position themselves as the leader of Zol Stria, so they can gain their own advantages over all of the Houses." She paused for a moment. "I have a better idea."

I looked over at Andres and Eliana, who gave me reassuring looks. Then I turned to Lex and Bjorn. They were all focused on Jenna, eager to hear what she had to say next. I turned my attention to her.

"So listen up, my bredren. We're going to get the rest of the relics back." Her Jamaican accent was thick and reassuring. "That way, when the Council is in possession of all of them, they won't come looking for you as the culprit." Her eyes landed on me with those last few words, then she turned back to the others. "We'll all be recognized as the heroes who saved Zol Stria, and they'll be figuring out why the vision didn't work like they expected. I mean, who knows? It's been a long time since they did the last cihuatl ceremony. If the stars have taught me anything, it's that we must be willing to accept change. To adapt and be flexible in the face of an evolving world. If this is what they teach, then the Council must accept that these are different times. Maybe that was a vision of you returning all the relics. Maybe you were planning to take them from him and return them to Zol Stria. Maybe it was the exact opposite of what we all think we saw. We have to be open to any possibility."

I wanted to believe her. I really did. "But how are we supposed to get all the relics back? We don't have any strong leads as to their exact location."

"No, we don't. But we don't have much of a choice. You're now a fugitive. The best place for you to hide is outside of Zol Stria until we get those relics back," Zayne said, and I nodded in agreement.

CHAPTER 4

Bjorn moved to my side, his massive rock-like arm brushing against mine. "If you're crossing the Gates, I'm crossing with you," he said. His amber eyes gave away a hint of concern on his ruthless warrior face.

"Me too," Jenna said.

Then Axel, Eliana, Andres, and Lex said, "Us too."

My chest squeezed as I took them all in. This was my unit. This was my family.

"Ok, ok, now I have to say I'm going too, or it just looks bad," Zayne added with the corners of his mouth turned up.

I gave him a sideways smirk.

Andres poured another round, and Jenna and I got started heating up spinach-and-artichoke dip that we had in the freezer from the last time we were here, along with setting out some tortilla chips to go with it. We agreed on making a beef brisket with cornbread for dinner, considering we had to get our energy up for the long trip out of the Gates that we had ahead of us.

I went to freshen up in the bathroom and found Eliana right outside the door as I was about to leave.

"Hey," Eliana said. "There's something I thought you should know."

I stopped in the hallway. "Go ahead..."

"So you know how I was dating that guy, the heir of House Aquarius?" Her face turned serious, and I knew this wasn't about her hooking up with him. This was something more.

"Yeah. I remember."

"Well, he said he saw Ixia. He was at the botanist looking at some new vanity elixirs they just got in, and he said she was there working with the head botanist. When he asked the Aquarius Council about it, they said she was reassigned there. It seems to me she was never exiled." Eliana blew out a breath.

"What? A traitor who stole their precious relics. How in the actual fuck is this even possible?" My voice sharpened.

"They wouldn't tell him anything else, but he told me he would ask around. That was right before this all happened with the vision."

"I'm going to have to tell Damian." My gaze shifted to the floor as I wrung my hands together. "That won't be a fun conversation."

"I know. I wonder what she could have done to get back in their good graces." Eliana shrugged.

I shook my head in disgust. "Thanks for telling me. Right now, everything is just so...stinky. And confusing. Maybe if I shower, I'll at least only be confused."

She nodded.

When we were all sitting and having dinner, some at the table and a few others at the countertop bar, I wondered how I had ended up with this great team around me. I considered myself lucky to count myself among them.

"What do we know about the relics?" Andres said in his smooth Cuban accent as he topped off my glass of wine.

There were six relics in total, each made from the pieces of the body of the UnZol King to suppress his power and bound him to an eternity inside the Void.

"I mean I know the Blade Bone went missing three decades ago, and the Council never realized it because it was replaced with such a high-quality counterfeit that no one suspected it was missing. What about the others?" Andres asked.

The Blade Bone was a piece of the UnZol King's rib cage, and it enabled the holder to travel through time. They could go forward in time as far as they wanted, but they could only go back in time to the moment they actually acquired the relic.

"The Devil's Eye and the Stone Mind went missing the same year as the Faellen Wars, 2012. It was the end of the Mayan calendar, when the factions of the Underworld divided. The rift damaged the chamber where the relics were held and there was a huge breach of security, which is when someone got to them. After our battle with Ixia, we retrieved the Stone Mind. Yet, the Devil's Eye is still missing," Zayne's light brown eyes seemed to darken as he explained.

The Devil's Eye was one of the UnZol King's eyes, and it allowed the holder to watch others, wherever and whenever they wanted. It essentially gave them the powers we sought at the Wall of Mirrors. But it was even more powerful in that it would allow the holder to see the motivations and desires of the people in the visions. It could also see through wards and deflector spells. Ixia had had the Stone Mind, which gave the holder the ability to conjure earthquakes, volcanic eruptions and shift the Earth's plates. We had fought Ixia to near-death back in Miami to retrieve that relic from her.

"Trent said that he was sure Solana had at least one of them, and maybe even both, otherwise she never would have given him the Blood Ruby," I added.

The Blood Ruby summoned the elements to create mass destruction. Solana had given it to Trent, and he had given it to us to defeat Ixia. Knowing that all these relics came from one man made me wonder how powerful the UnZol King actually was. *How could one man's body parts command so much vast, utter power?*

"And the other relics, still in the possession of the Council, are the Obsidian Heart and Snake Tongue," I chimed in.

"So, let's start with Solana. She either has the Devil's Eye or the Blade Bone. Whatever relic she has, we'll use its power to track down and retrieve the other. Then we will have the two missing relics to return to the Council," Lex explained.

"Well, that's brilliant. It only took having Sasha's life at risk for us to work on getting those relics back." Bjorn laughed, and when he did his massive chest and arms shook in unison.

"We just needed the right motivation," Jenna said, handing me the shot that Andres had just poured.

"To our latest mission. Retrieve the relics and get the Council off our backs," Andres said decidedly, and we all lifted our cups and kicked back the shots in one gulp.

The tart whisky burned as it went down, the spicy beverage awakening my senses. As it settled, I realized how much my unit meant to me. It wasn't lost on me that Andres had said "get the Council off our backs" instead of "off Sasha's back." He said this as though what was happening right now was happening to all of us. This unit was my home, and some vision from the cihuatl wouldn't ruin it. I would protect us, and what we had, with my life.

CHAPTER 5

U nder the cover of night, a day later and through the back streets, we arrived at Sagittarius Gate. This was the strangest and least occupied Zodiac Gate of them all. There were rumors that Fae who crossed this Gate never returned. I managed to sneak out of this Gate once to visit Trent, and it was anything but easy to do, which was why I realized no one ever went that way. Another reason no one came through this Gate was because it opened up into a remote jungle in Venezuela, making it very hard to travel once you got to the other side.

But even still, this place looked creepy. The Gate was at the bottom of a massive sinkhole that must have formed thousands of years ago, because there was a whole forest at the bottom of the sinkhole, just outside the Gate. Unless you had wings or air magic, the only way down the sinkhole was by way of a rope hanging off the side, because Sagittarius House had never invested in stairs or an elevator. This was probably because going up and down the sinkhole wasn't a problem for the winged Fae of House Sagittarius. The Fae of this House were all manner of centaurs that could fly with ease up and down the side. It was common knowledge that the Fae of Sagittarius simply never wanted to visit the humans on the other side of the Gate. But like most of the light-energy Fae, the centaurs slept at night, whereas the dark was the nagual's playground.

Five of us traveled together: me, Jenna, Lex, Bjorn and Zayne. Even after all those fine sentiments, we agreed that Andres, Eliana and Axel needed to stay behind as our eyes and ears in Zol Stria. They would keep a low profile while we went on our mission, learning what they could about the Council's plans for me while gaining any intel they could to help us. Tension built in my chest as I worried that they were putting themselves in danger just for my sake. Whenever I told Jenna what I was thinking, she just told me to "get over myself." They weren't having it.

Two centaurs stood guard upon our arrival at the wall that surrounded the sinkhole. Their bows and arrows were slung over their shoulders, a second away from their grasp. When provoked, the centaurs were known to draw the most precise and deadly bows in all of Zol Stria. And yet still, they were standing at the wall entirely unaware of our presence.

"The guards never gave me a hard time before. I think these guys are slackers and they haven't gotten word yet to look for me," I offered, hoping I was right.

Zayne said, "Bjorn, let's just walk up as if it was any normal Gate crossing. If they give us trouble, we attack. If they don't, then the rest of you walk behind us all casual."

Under the cover of trees and bushes, the rest of us watched them gain access to the Gate without issue. They emerged on the path, and we strolled behind them shortly after. I felt the gaze of the younger centaur on me a few breaths longer than what I'd expected. Jenna had cast a spell to turn my hair pink, but it wasn't very strong and would only last long enough for me to cross. I couldn't cast hair-color spells like she did.

The younger centaur was smoking a cigarette and blew the smoke toward me as I walked by him.

"No one comes this way on a new moon. It's pitch black down there. Good luck finding your way," the older one with the scruffy beard called out after we passed him. The both of them chuckled and turned, following us slowly, as though curious. They exchanged whispers, and I tried to ignore them.

Bjorn drew from his earth magic to create thick and sturdy vines for us to climb down. One by one we descended, my hands grasping and releasing the vines as I went. The threads burned my skin. I looked up and saw the centaurs staring at us from over the rim, watching our descent. My legs pushed off the mossy rock. Jenna used air magic to support her way down, but she still used the rope to keep her steady.

"I forgot to tell you, he wakes up every new moon," the young centaur yelled down at us.

"Who? Who wakes up?" Lex looked over at me and asked as the centaurs laughed from above.

"I don't know. Never crossed this Gate during a new moon," I ground out under my breath.

It was dark, and even though our night vision was better than most Fae, it wasn't perfect, and it was much harder without the light of the moon. I drew flames to my hands whenever I could to cast light for us. I felt the soft ground under my boots when I finally made it to the bottom and began to open and close my hands to shake off the soreness of holding that rope. I brought a bright fire to both my hands to light the forest up and make our way to where I knew the heavy iron door was.

When we got to the entrance, it was covered by all manner of fallen branches, leaves and sticks. Some storm must have blown through here since I last came. By the look of this sinkhole, it seemed it could flood if there were heavy rains.

I heard a rustle in the leaves beyond, but I couldn't see anything. We were not alone.

"Did you guys hear that?" I asked.

"Yeah, I heard it. What is it?" Jenna said, her eyes wide as she searched the dark foliage.

"Bjorn, help me. Let's get this rusty door open," Zayne said. He pushed away the shrubbery blocking the Gate and began to yank at the handle to the heavy iron door.

"It's got tentacles," I said, still staring at the forest as long black limbs pushed away the branches. I could smell the beast's wretched breath when it opened a wide mouth and grunted out a roar. Its mouth was the size of a hippo, its teeth as long as daggers. "And from what I can tell, this creature means to eat us." My voice was urgent now. I had never passed through here during a new moon, and those idiots up there thought it was funny not to warn us what we'd be walking into.

This was a kizer. I had read about them; they weighed at least four tons. I shrugged off my backpack, threw off my shoes and pants and yanked off my shirt. I set it all down by the door and shifted the moment a tentacle swept toward me. Jenna and Lex had already shifted and were taking their positions at its side.

This was why the centaur guards were whispering and chuckling. They knew exactly what we would be walking into. Well at least now we knew the centaurs weren't aware that we were currently Zol Stria's most wanted, otherwise they wouldn't have risked us like this. But it was obvious now that they didn't care much for the nagual protectors. Although we were known as the protectors of Zol Stria, some Fae-types took issue with the status that gave us, and challenged that they were in fact, better warriors than we were. The centaurs were definitely among those that felt that way.

Jenna had an appendage latched between her fangs, and Lex was in position to lunge onto the land-octopus's back. It had four elephant-like legs that held a body the size of a small house, with six octopus-like tentacles. The beast thrashed at Jenna, banging her against a tree. But she was as tough as nails and could handle it. I made a quick calculation: if Lex was coming at her from behind, then he would expect me to flank on the right. But there were just way too many tentacles reaching for me to have any chance of getting there.

I ducked and leapt as quickly as I could and made it to the right, three tentacles reaching for me. Perfect. As I wove around them, I noticed I was leading it away from Zayne and Bjorn so they could get that damn door open. Jenna was holding its attention at its left just as Lex made it onto its back. He dug his fangs into the thick, rubbery flesh, and crimson blood oozed out over its head. This made it even angrier, and it knocked trees over as it tried to shake him off. But he dug his claws in hard and didn't release his grip on its neck. I made a leap for the kizer's jaw but missed, the creature moving too quickly even for my reflexes. Instead I wrapped my teeth around another of its tentacles, feeling my fangs sink deep into flesh. Its thrashing began to slow, and within a few seconds it stopped completely and began to back away.

I just want to leave.

I didn't hear these words as much as I felt them. The creature spoke with a strange vibration against the inside of my skull. I released the tentacle from between my teeth and gave Jenna a look. She hesitated, then released her grip on it also.

I've been trapped here for over a hundred moons. I want to leave.

The tremor of these words swept across my skin as I studied the creature's energy. Its energy was more organized than other creatures I'd seen, and from what I could tell, it wasn't trying to deceive us. I shifted back to my Zol skin.

"It says it wants to leave. Did you guys hear that?" I said as I stood completely naked in front of the panting beast.

Lex released his hold on top and looked at me, his green eyes glowing and the snarl on his face relaxing. Jenna glanced over at me, too, and nodded. Her feline eyes told me she had heard something as well. I held my hands up in a show of peace.

Lex nodded as though he had felt something too.

"Jenna, Zayne, do you guys think you could lift it up and out of here with air and water?"

Jenna, still in her jaguar form, shook her head. I looked over at Zayne, who had managed to crack the door open slightly by pushing on it with his shoulder. He stopped, and Bjorn immediately took his place and kept shoving the door, releasing it a centimeter at a time.

"I don't know, Sasha. It's big. It would take at least three air elementals to get it out. Water won't do much of anything," Zayne answered as he went back to helping Bjorn.

Lex leapt off the kizer and shifted, not a drop of sweat on his dark-brown skin.

"Why are you even down here? Is this some sort of punishment?" Lex asked.

The kizer took several steps back and disappeared into the forest.

"What was that about?" Lex looked to me, and I shrugged. "It's been banished down here for a reason, Sasha."

"Wait. Maybe not. What if it fell and got stuck and just can't get out? I feel really bad for it." I reached for my clothes and hesitated.

"Come on, we got it," Zayne yelled, and we darted back to the Gate. I hoped we hadn't harmed the beast too badly. It had some scratches, but it would be fine.

"Guys, can one of you carry my pack for me? I think I'll go the rest of the way in my jaguar. She wants to run," I told them.

"I got it," Bjorn said as he grabbed my pack.

"Same here. Running," Lex said.

"Me too," Jenna said.

The three of us shifted into our jaguars just as Zayne and Bjorn grabbed our packs and clothing, and we made our way through the Gate.

CHAPTER 6

The other side of Sagittarius Gate was legit the middle of the jungle. There was nothing and no one around for miles. Zayne and Bjorn walked while I led the way with the other nagual as we ran ahead to the roads, searching for something to travel in. We found a decent truck and brought the guys straight to it. Zayne purchased it from the local villager with Venezuelan pesos we had brought with us. We stored local currency at our safe house precisely for moments like these. Once we made it to the nearest town with cell reception, we made a call.

It would be impossible to go to our familiar contacts for help, but we knew one person who didn't care at all about the rules of Zol Stria. My shaman, Damian. He was a master of staying off the grid. He had done it so well after all these years, and for once, I was glad he did.

"He'll probably turn us away," Lex said while we were on our way to his place. "He only cares about himself." I knew he was saying this because of the many years he abandoned his role as my shaman, and it almost cost me my life. But he had come around and even apologized for all that. Even still, the fact that he left Zol Stria again and refused to be a practicing Zol Shaman made me wonder.

I cut my eyes to him. I had to believe Damian would help us.

"Let's make a bet. If Damian sees us through this and proves he does care about us, I win. Loser owes the other one dinner at Zupita's Mexican Restaurant for a month." After everyone placed their bets, I was the only one that bet in favor of Damian pulling through to the end.

One day later, we arrived at his hacienda in the Sierra Nevada Mountains of Colombia.

"Were you followed?" Damian asked me when we arrived at his large, gated estate, concern dotting his eyes. He was just as I remembered him, his beard was impeccably groomed, and his hair brushed neatly in place.

Over the past three years in the Academy, we had kept in touch. He sent me updates and continued to search for Ixia, who had been exiled from Zol

Stria after stealing the Stone Mind. Damian had purchased a winery here in the mountains, and it felt forgotten by the world. As we approached, I could sense thick wards around the rolling hills that made up his estate, released only as we were granted entry at the guard post.

"No, we went through Sagittarius Gate, and now we know why no one ever travels through there," Bjorn answered him, and a shudder raced down my spine at the memory of the poor creature trapped down there.

"It's a miracle I got through when I did that one time," I said.

"Have you picked up anything? The Council is going to know we came here. I think we're a few days ahead of their tactical teams," Zayne said. The five of us had spilled into a sitting room, but no one sat. "We can't stay."

"You won't be staying," a familiar voice said. Trent took two steps out of the shadowy hallway.

I hadn't sensed his presence in the slightest. I gasped at the sight of him. His beard, slightly thicker now; his hair full and loose, falling just below his ears but just as golden as I remembered; his blue eyes penetrating in contrast with his bronze skin.

"Today, my horoscope said I would be busy arranging and bringing people together, and look, here we are." His eyes revealed a hint of playful glimmer, but the corners of his mouth curled only slightly upward.

I gasped and dropped my backpack on the floor. My body compelled me toward him, first with slow steps, then closing the gap between us in three quick paces. Now just a step away, I stopped myself from reaching my arms around him, just so I could search his eyes for the man I loved. Was he still there, underneath this whole mafia-boss vibe he was giving off?

He took my face in his right hand as he gently caressed my jaw, then my neck. His fangs snapped out with a snarl. I didn't even flinch. That was a vampire's way of showing they wanted you, and I wanted him to want me. To want all of me. But he restrained himself and didn't bite.

"I missed you," I managed to breathe out as I rested my hands on his unyielding chest, ignoring the empty glare of his predatory vampire eyes. He quickly retracted his fangs and released his deflector spell, just as I released mine, so our energy could interlace.

"I missed you too. And there's no way you're ending up as the wife of some UnZol Asshole King or whatever it is they call him. You are mine," he said, then leaned in to meet his lips to mine.

Instantly my body responded, heating at the center. My desire for him was kindled by the fire of our kiss as I felt the contrast of his soft lips, his rough beard and sharp teeth grazing against my flesh. That was all it took to make me want to lose myself in him. But now wasn't the time. I don't know how I managed to do it, but I pulled myself away. I glanced up at him and he gave me a soft smile. Then the lines of his lips straightened.

"We're leaving right now. Zol Stria will know you've come here, and they will send their hounds. Come with me. We're going to Louisiana," he said. His suit was immaculate, and he smelled of orange and spice. He stood tall, as if he was used to giving commands and having others obey him.

"Why Louisiana? What's there?" I asked, suddenly aware of the others. They knew all about Trent, and Jenna knew exactly how I felt about him. And because he'd helped us retrieve the Blood Ruby on our last mission, they trusted him.

"Because in Louisiana I have access to a safe house with an ancient ward set to the Transit of Venus of 1876. It's unbreakable, and only two people know of the location—me and an old vampire friend of mine who's currently vacationing on his yacht off the coast of the Maldives. He owes me a favor. No one is even going to think of looking for you there. We'll have a place to lay low until we figure out a plan." Even though he had turned to face the rest of the group, his hand never left my waist.

I tried to read their faces, and they began to turn to each other in silent exchanges of uncertainty. We were on the run, and it sucked to be figuring things out as we went along, but we didn't have much choice.

"Someone is going to come looking for us here. They're probably already on their way," I insisted.

"Not likely. I've got my own wards on this place. You're the only ones to know about it," Damian said. "But you've left a trail here. They could track you, and besides, I've left a trail of my own over the years in town. If they go asking around and track me, eventually they will find you. Trent's suggestion sounds good. I checked it out, and the wards are unlike anything I've ever seen. Those ancient vampires knew what they were doing." Damian shoved his hands in his pockets and leaned against the wall. "From there, we can go anywhere in the world. Trent has a private jet."

As I stood next to Trent and thought about being with him on his luxury private jet for the flight to Louisiana, I was suddenly much more conscious of how much of a hot, sweaty mess I was after hiking through hours of jungle to get to the unairconditioned truck that brought us here. In that moment, I was so grateful that vampires couldn't read minds.

"Can I at least shower first?" Jenna asked, seeming to read my mind.

"Me too," Eliana and I said at the same time.

"A two-minute boot-camp shower is all we have time for. My pilot is waiting on the air strip." Trent gave my shoulders a reassuring squeeze.

The three of us scrambled, pushing each other out of the way as we poked our heads in doors in the hallway in search of a shower.

"Me first." I shoved Jenna.

"No, me." She shoved me back.

"There are four showers, no need to fight over them," Damian huffed and pointed them out for us before returning to the main room.

Jenna jumped into the first shower she saw, and I walked with Eliana as she entered a large guest bathroom with dark wood cabinets and marble finishes. She glanced over at me before closing the door behind her and said with a wink, "Girl, I know exactly why you want to shower so bad."

"Is it that obvious?" I laughed as I turned to leave.

I made my way to a bathroom in another guest room two doors down. As I took in the high-end finishes, the frameless shower with floor-to-ceiling porcelain tile, I took in a deep breath to steady my racing mind. As I undressed to enter the shower, I realized that I still hadn't told Damian what Eliana told me about Ixia. As the warm water poured over my head, I lifted my chin so the shower would cascade directly on my face. I raised my hands to my cheeks and massaged them with foamy face wash. I was too tired and overwhelmed to even be outraged by the news Eliana shared about Ixia being taken back in by the Council. I mean, everything else had gone to shit, so why not that too?

On top of that, I hadn't expected to see Trent here, at Damian's. I had been working hard to keep my emotions in check since I had seen the vision about him. I kept any thoughts of panic and insecurity at bay by telling myself this was my path and that the stars had put me here for a reason. It was up to me to find my way out of it. And I'd never once considered that this path would lead me back into the arms of a mafia boss who worked for the Dark Zodiac. A mafia boss who happened to be the man I loved.

No matter which way I turned, trouble seemed to find me.

Good thing I'm not afraid of trouble.

CHAPTER 7

Becoming a nagual meant I was a badass who could summon the power of the shadows in order to take down the forces that wanted to unleash depraved evil on the world. But it didn't mean I didn't get tired. As excited as I was to see Trent, and as much as I had planned to join the mile-high club with him in his private jet, I fell asleep within seconds of takeoff. The combination of the smooth, beige-leather recliner with the descent of the evening sun was enough to knock me out like a light. I slept the entire way there. Apparently I missed the meal, but Trent told me he would get me something when we arrived at the home where we were staying.

By the time we landed in New Orleans, I was well rested and fully recovered. We took many precautions, even switching cars on the way to the waterfront home in the city. I managed to sit next to Damian on the drive and tell him what I had learned about Ixia. He had no reaction, no outrage or visible anger. It was as though I was telling him we were out of coffee. He just shook his head and gazed out the window, devoid of emotion.

We were on our way to one of the many vacation homes owned by Trent's billionaire client. Trent had told his client he was in the market to buy a home in the area so his client had invited him to stay there while he searched.

White wood and grey stones were an ongoing theme throughout the five-bedroom, five-bath contemporary home. Trent walked me to one of the two master bedrooms on the upper level. The large bed faced a glass wall of sliding doors overlooking miles of open water. I took a deep breath in, as though I could finally relax. Without a sound, Trent moved to stand behind me. I didn't turn around, but instead kept my eyes fixed on the endless horizon.

"This will be your room," he said. "And I plan for us to do a whole lot of inappropriate things in here." I heard his fangs snap out again as he trailed a finger along my neck.

My cheeks felt flush. "How inappropriate, exactly?" I bit my lower lip.

"As inappropriate as it gets."

I had missed hearing his smooth voice. I missed the comfort of having him next to me. I missed the way he touched me. Warmth grew in my chest. I was ready to forget every doubt I'd ever had about him. About us.

I turned around and ran my hand along his chest, pursing my lips slightly. "I'd like to get some food in me first and check on the others, make sure everything is ok. Get to know my exit strategy, that sort of thing." I angled my head. I felt torn about my feelings for him and lost on how to navigate our two very different worlds.

"That's fair. I'll show you around." He took my hand in his and began the tour.

Room after room was perfectly decorated with the local gilded-and-tufted country antiques, emphasizing its contemporary feel. Elaborate ceiling medallions were tastefully placed among simpler beige or white furniture pieces to keep the look from being overwhelming. After getting clear on the house layout, its entrances and exits, and knowing where I could find everyone, I felt more at ease. He was right that there was plenty of room for all of us.

By the end of our tour, the others had settled in their rooms, also tired from the long day. Bjorn stepped into the hallway while we were on our way to the kitchen, the mass of him taking up the whole space in front of us. He glared at Trent, and after our many days of training together, I knew that expression.

Bjorn's eyes met mine. "Sasha, you trust Trent and we trust you." I nodded. Bjorn took a step forward and stood a hand's space away from Trent. He looked down at him; Trent was a few inches shorter than Bjorn and easily half his mass. "Don't make us regret it."

Trent returned his cold stare, his face unreadable. "I would never, ever do anything to hurt Sasha or the people she loves. You can trust me."

Bjorn chewed his lip, as though considering what Trent had said as his eyes scanned from me to Trent, who stood completely motionless in front of him as only a vampire could do. He then turned and left, tension still thick in the air.

Trent and I were alone in the kitchen. He had a meal ready of Kobo steak and fries with a bottle of Malbec. The perfect pairing.

"You sure you don't want a bite?" I asked him. If vampires had to survive without blood, they could consume rare steak and cooked vegetables. But eating like that would only last a few weeks before failing to give them the nutrients they needed. Soon after their bodies would suffer from malnutrition. Still, I knew Trent loved a good cut of meat.

"Oh, I certainly do. But I'm saving my appetite," he said, his eyes concentrated on me.

My chest heaved as I took another bite. It was a little strange, being so close to him again, on the run like this. After a few more bites and a sip of wine, I gently set down my utensils and lifted the napkin from my lap. *He's here, and I'm here. And it's been way too long.*

I reached for his hand just as he moved to stand from the table. He towered over me while reaching his hand around my waist and pulling me up off my chair and closer to him. He awakened all my senses as he encircled me, and I forgot every frustration and worry about our time apart.

His fingers pressed urgently into my side as his lips met mine once again, bringing that familiar heat to pool between my legs. He drew his gaze from my lips to my eyes. In another instant I watched as his fangs snapped out while he compulsively pulled my hair to the side to reveal my neck. I fought against the heat of our connection and took one step back.

"Wait. Not here. Let's go to the room," I said.

Disappointment rolled across his face. I had to purse my lips together to keep myself from laughing. Now that he had control of both the Miami Mafia and the Colombian Cartel, he wasn't used to not getting what he wanted the moment he wanted it.

"It's adorable watching you pout," I giggled as we approached the bedroom.

He closed the door with a smooth hand and, I was sure, a rock-solid hard-on in his pants. And I hoped that was the last calm and controlled movement I would see from him for the rest of the night.

We returned to the bedroom's king bed with fluffy Euro-style pillows. A dark-navy wall was the focus of the room, and against it rested a light-colored, tufted headboard. White curtains framed the sliding doors to a balcony overlooking the Gulf of Mexico. But right now, none of the decor of the room mattered. I hadn't turned to him yet, instead wandering around and looking behind curtains and extending my awareness outside. Although I had toured the house, one could never be too careful. I kept checking and sensing nothing, and that was what I'd hoped for. I lifted a powerful deflector spell that merged with his and extended it out the patio door. I felt his eyes on me, and finally I turned to face him from where I was standing, across the room.

His fangs jutted out of his mouth, and he stood there, revealing himself to me. This creature that he had become, a monster that fed off others. The last time I had seen him he had told me how much he hated the undeniable urge he had to feed. How the very people he'd once signed up to protect as a SERE in the military were now the same people he wanted to drain. His new power and ability tormented him. Yet somehow, from the way he looked right now, it didn't seem like he was tormented at all. In fact, I noticed something different about him. He seemed to embody the very thing he had resisted all this time.

And no matter how much I tried to convince him to come to Zol Stria and join other Zol Vampires that had found a less murderous way to live, he refused.

He had been turned by a Dark Vampire, and he had his reasons. Of course, his reasoning was that he wanted to stay close to Solana as a spy on the inside. But I believed he also enjoyed his role as a mafia boss and all that unchecked power it gave him. After all, he was incredibly good at it.

He darted with his vampire speed and in the blink of an eye stood before me. Gently and with restraint, he swept my hair back and leaned closer. I felt only his warm breath prickle my skin. My eyes opened wide just as my mouth parted. A small gasp left my throat as his fangs sank in and my body gave way to his deep pulling. I missed being this way. His venom was addictive, and I was completely hooked. My knees buckled under his embrace. My shoulders dropped.

It has been way too long since I've felt him.

As he drew blood from my veins, it was as though there was a string that went from all the way down my center to the apex of my thighs, and it was almost like he was pulling from those blood vessels directly.

All I want is to fill myself with him. He is everything.

I pressed my hands against his firm chest and reached for the contours of his hard lines inside his shirt at his sides. The only thought in my mind was him. Desperately, my hand shifted into his pants, eager to feel the length of him under my palm.

But just then my head began to spin, and my hands felt weak. I brought them up to his firm chest and pushed myself off of him, his fangs sliding out of my neck. "I have to sit down." I stumbled back and made my way to the bed. My hooded eyes met his, and I tilted my head as I realized he had a predatory gaze locked on me. He wiped blood from his lips as I reached my hand up to my neck. Then it hit me: he had taken too much blood.

"What are you doing?" My voice was soft and raspy, but my mind was on the defensive. Had he changed sides? I couldn't believe I was still doubting him, but I remembered the lessons I'd learned along the way. *Trust no one.*

He wiped the stone-cold-killer look off of his face and gave me a half-smile just as he unbuttoned his designer Italian shirt. "I'm coming for you," he said, and darted in front of me again.

To trust him now, with everything going on, made me feel vulnerable. I didn't have the protection of Zol Stria. Right now, all I had was my unit, which also included Damian and him. He looked down at me and cradled my jaw in his hand. I closed my eyes and leaned into him. My eyes opened to slits as I pressed my lips against his bare abdomen. The strong contours of his abs brought out something savage in me, and I no longer felt dizzy. Now I was famished, and he was the only thing that could satiate me. My tongue met his skin, and he released a soft groan.

My fingers opened the top button of his pants, and I had him in my hold, then my lips met his fully erect flesh. The moisture of my mouth and tongue were making him grow longer and thicker. My head moved in a steady rhythm as my hands massaged the bottom. Steady and smooth, he gasped and moaned in the way only a very powerful vampire could.

"I want to feel you," he growled and reached his hands to my sides, lifting me with him on the bed, gathering me in his arms. His muscles contracted around me as he laid me down, my head resting on the large pillow. My center grew warmer with every passing instant. I writhed with desire, my skin thrummed against his touch, my blood coursed with need of him. His hands moved along my sides; his fangs extended again.

"Don't. Not again. You'll drain me."

He stared at me, confusion lacing his eyes. As though he hadn't even realized what he was doing, unaware of the beast he was. Now he unbuttoned my pants and slid them off. I had grown moist already, and his fingers met my center, pressing there, ever aware of exactly what he needed to do, how I had to feel. There was nowhere else to be in this very moment. Nothing other than the complete satisfaction of his touch. I shuddered as his fingers moved the thin fabric of my panties to the side, and I responded to his touch with a loud moan. I grew wetter and ached for him. All of him.

My hips rocked in response to his touch just as his lips met my neck, my ear, my cheek, my lips. My tongue reached for his, and I felt his chest heave. His touch wasn't warm, but it did warm me. I had enough fire for both of us until it was too hot. I was too wet. He entered me just then, right when I couldn't take just his fingers anymore. I wrapped my legs around him, rocking into him, connecting my body with his, deeper and deeper. It was everything I needed. All I wanted was for everything else in our lives to stop existing so we could go on like this forever. My breath came in faster, my heart pounded, and I threw my head back as I crossed over the edge of my desire as he thrusted himself inside me, pounding and rocking to our own enchanted rhythm until the convulsion between my legs stopped.

He lay on his back, his penetrating eyes telling me he wanted more. I released a shaky breath and licked my lips. "We aren't done," he said in a tone that was so fucking sexy and commanding all at once. I climbed on top of him, my body slick with the heat of our connection.

His lips met my breast, stimulating my every nerve and making my nipple hard under his soft tongue. I released a loud moan as pleasure rocked through my body, arching my back when he moved his mouth to the other breast. When he lifted his head, I shifted on top of his manhood, and I moved my hips up and down on his erection until he pushed it inside with a series of thrusts. Up and down, I moved my body faster and faster as I gripped his arms and became overwhelmed with the need of him. He released a loud moan of his own, his body tightening as we finished at the same moment. He began to relax next to me, and the feverish desire between us quelled, at least for now.

CHAPTER 8

I awoke to an empty bed and a welcome soreness between my legs. The sun was high in the sky; I could tell by the bright light that entered the small cracks between the door to the balcony and the blackout curtains. My heart began to race the moment I awoke, ever aware of my current state as a fugitive of Zol Stria. The Zol Fae believed in balance. Maybe they wouldn't come after me. Maybe they would "wait in stillness," as the Zol Sen would say, rather than react to the situation. Maybe that's why we were able to cross Sagittarius Gate unscathed.

My brain continued its internal banter as I showered and changed into black jeans, a dark-green tank top and a fitted cotton jacket I had found in the closet. I'd also found a pair of lace-up boots that were just my size.

I made my way downstairs, following the smell of fresh eggs, bacon and potatoes. Bjorn must be cooking. He made the most delicious breakfast I had ever tasted.

"There's nothing sexier than a man who knows how to cook," I said, smiling as I entered the kitchen. Then I searched the cabinets for a coffee mug. Jenna, Zayne and Trent were already there, and Lex was coming down the stairs right after me.

"All part of my secret plan to steal you away from Trent," Bjorn joked as a playful smile graced his face. I grabbed a plate and, after he served me, planted a kiss on his cheek.

Trent was sitting at a small table by the window, having a cup of coffee, his mind off somewhere else. His gaze distant.

"When did you have time to shop for all these new clothes?" I asked as I sat down next to him.

He turned to me, his movements ever calm and controlled. "Yesterday, as soon as I heard you were leaving Zol Stria. Damian told me you guys brought very little with you so I took the liberty. I bought several different sizes of everything, just in case." His eyes almost flashed turquoise as they fell upon me.

"I'm glad you did." I smiled. His hand rested on my thigh under the table.

"So am I, even though the underwear you got me is too tight," Lex said. He gave Jenna a wink, and she giggled.

"Oh, so you need big-boy undies now?" Trent joked, a smile cracking his face.

When we finished eating, Bjorn and Zayne hit the gym, Jenna and Lex retreated to their room, and Damian did whatever Damian does while Trent and I took another reprieve in our bedroom. It was even more charged than the night before. A few hours later, when I had finished swimming in bedsheets, I was ready to face reality. Damian then called us to the dining room to strategize.

"Brother, we appreciate your hospitality," Zayne said. "And as far as vampires go, it's hard for me to say this, but we're putting our trust in you. After all, you gave us the Blood Ruby and you fought with us when Ixia tried to take us all out. But we've got a lot at stake and we need to ask you something." Zayne's eyes were focused on Trent, who ran a hand through his golden hair. "How did you get Solana to look past your losing the Blood Ruby? She's not known for overlooking things. Especially not something this major. I would have expected you to have limbs severed or even killed for something like that."

That familiar raging heat singed my chest at the very thought of Trent working for Solana. Zayne was forcing me to face something I didn't want to face.

"Solana and I have... a special relationship." Trent was standing across the table from me and choosing his words carefully. A faint inky mist surrounded him, and because of his immortal state, there was no aura.

"Really, what kind of relationship?" I pressed him.

"I only did it to protect you. All of you." His eyes scanned the room, landing on me. "She's gained control of five major mafias and has managed to convince many of them to join her because of the supernatural protection she offers. Years ago I had wondered how she was doing it, until I learned about the relics. I do believe she has both the Blade Bone and the Devil's Eye. Which is how she's gotten away with so much. Between time travel and seeing the target's operation, she has a huge advantage. With the Blade Bone she can influence small but very precise moments in time, which allow her to take over each new territory she's after. And she can watch them all with the Devil's Eye, anticipating their next move. Which is why I knew I had to stay close to her... With these relics, she's dangerously powerful."

His gaze fell on me, and my heart dropped.

"How close?" I asked. I didn't really want to know the answer, but I had to face what I suspected, which was that he was sleeping with her.

"Like I said, we have a special relationship." His face darkened, but his expression gave nothing away. If this bothered him, if he thought he had done something wrong, his face didn't show it. "Because of our relationship, she gave me a chance to explain. I told her I was at the warehouse gathering intel for retaliation on the attack on us the night of the art exhibition. I told her that the combination of the Stone Mind, and the power of the seven nagual and a shaman, would overpower the Blood Ruby. All of this was true. It helped that she knew Ixia. She studied under her at the Academy. She knows exactly how powerful she is..."

I glared at him. I wished he would come out and say what we were all thinking.

Jenna's expression softened when I looked at her. She knew me well enough to know that my heart was on the brink of shattering into a thousand pieces as I imagined him in the thrall of the savage queen of the Dark Zodiac.

"Just say it, Trent. Just come out and say it. You know I hate it when people try and cover things up. And what I hate worst of all is being lied to. Let's just call a spade a spade. You're sleeping with her." My eyes must have had flames in them, because I could feel my fire element rising. "Say it!"

I couldn't take it anymore. I had to know. Right here. Right now. In front of the people I trusted most in the entire world. In all my fury I could not control the fire from rising into my fists.

"Yes. I've slept with her a few times." A vulnerable, hurt expression flashed over his face. This wasn't something he was proud of. "At first, I did it to protect you. To gather intel, just like we'd talked about. But she didn't believe anything I told her. She has the Devil's Eye—with it, she can see the truth of anything and everything. And she saw it all. There is no hiding from Solana."

Every set of nagual eyes pierced into Trent, and I felt my own jaguar stir beneath the surface. Along with a rage-filled heat that bubbled up like lava in my chest.

Every part of me that once thought he was mine was nothing less than completely crushed. I turned away so he wouldn't see the tears welling in my eyes. My jaguar itched to be released, and it took all of my strength to keep her from unleashing all over him. I slapped warm tears off my cheeks as I dashed out the back door. *How could I be so stupid?* Of course he was sleeping with her. That was why she kept him close and allowed him to have so much power. I was just too in love with him to accept the writing on the wall. So stupid that Zayne needed to call him out just so I would see the truth of the man I loved.

I stepped onto the hot and humid patio and ripped my clothes off the instant I was outside, urgently claiming the dark energy from every crevice of the wooded area around me. Hungry for an adrenaline-filled rush of power, the dark mist filled me just as I shifted seamlessly into my jaguar form. Waves of shadows coiled around me, and I released the feral beast that I'd kept tightly controlled through every word that had come out of Trent's mouth. She and I were now one, and I ran with the power of the darkness and the shadows. The monsters that many moons ago had paralyzed me with fear were now my energy source, and they gave me all the power I needed to run for miles. Faster than any creature in Zol Stria, including the vampire.

So fast he couldn't catch me to explain, even if he tried.

—·—

CHAPTER 9

My heart hammered in my chest as I ran until my large paws couldn't carry me anymore. They were sore from the rocks, stubble and branches that broke under each of my heavy steps. I ran over ten miles into the deep forest outside of the city, careful to go unseen as I left the suburban neighborhood, sticking to the shadows and easily avoiding the humans that radiated color with their auras on full display around them everywhere they went. I had gotten so used to the retracted auras of Zol Stria that humans had become even more obvious in their emotions and just as ridiculously easy to read.

I ran so far without truly tracking where I was going, and before I realized it I was in the middle of the woods. The cool air was refreshing against my jaguar's fur. I wouldn't shift back into a human here. But I would take my time in clearing my mind.

My hot vampire boyfriend was sleeping with another woman, and there was no way he was doing it just to protect us. He must have enjoyed it. Her thick red hair. Her full round lips. Her amber eyes combined with her toned and curvy body were enough to drive any man crazy. Add to all of that the bond as his maker, and I was absolutely sure that some part of him was drawn to her. I didn't know why I'd even thought we could make this work.

And now I had to wonder if he would be willing to betray all of us just for her. Maybe he wanted to put us in this exact situation. My chest ached, and my mind was blurry. Nothing was clear anymore. He couldn't be trusted with my heart or my unit. *Shit. I just left him alone with the others.* I had to get them away from him! We would find some other way out of this mess.

As I paced around the rocks at the edge of a river, my mind continued to race. I considered our options. We could take our chances at Damian's or find another place to hide while we worked to retrieve the relics. At the very least, I could trust Damian.

Just as I turned to leave, I felt a powerful wind surge through the air. It was followed by a high-pitched squeal, one that could only come from the souls of the underworld. These sounds used to scare the shit out of me. Now, my ears perked up and I scanned the woods.

The sounds of the darkest, deranged, eternally damned souls got closer, and I took off running. No sense sticking around to find out what, or who, was after me.

As the sounds got louder and the wind blew colder, I sensed that it might not be just a powerful Fae. From the howl of the wind and the strength of the mist that began rolling in, I had a bad feeling it could be one of the twin gods. My creators and those that commanded me above all other gods.

When I had first encountered the gods during the transformation ritual, I had never felt such a powerful control over my entire being. It was as though my own mind had relinquished control of all my bodily functions. There was nothing I could do but sit and obey the commands of the gods as they completed the ceremony. It was both paralyzing and somehow freeing at the same time. The freedom came from the feeling of finally knowing my creator and understanding that all the confusing parts of my life made sense.

There was no one that could stop a nagual with their magical spells. No shaman or Fae that could cast any incantation that could harm our kind. Not in all those years of innovation in magic or alchemy did anyone find a way to use magic against us while we were in our jaguar form. Nothing other than the death gods who had created us. The twin Mayan gods, Hun-Cane and Vucub-Cane, could unleash enough power to control our kind. Nagual were so powerful we could even entirely subdue the magic of the relics of the UnZol King and render them useless. However, by nature we were designed so that we could never turn our power on the gods who had created us. I hadn't seen them since that transformational ritual, and I had forgotten how overpowering their presence was. And if one of those gods were here right now, I would have no choice but to bow to him. Then it occurred to me that if the death gods captured me, they would turn me into the Council. Something I was sure I did not want

And yet, no matter how fast I ran those unnatural sounds grew louder and closer. I cringed at the idea of what the death god wanted with me and what he could possibly do once he had me. I felt a tug at my core. It was a sinking feeling like no other; the passive call of my star-bound soul.

Gods like the twins could be anywhere at any time on Earth and Zol Stria. They were the bridge between our parallel worlds. They had created the Underworld prison, Xibalba. And as the creators, they were responsible for keeping the prisoners under control. And of all the five Underworlds, theirs was considered maximum security. They were the only one of the five factions that had not lost prisoners during the Faellen Wars. That's why the most notorious prisoners were spending eternity there. And that was why I knew that if the twin gods were coming for me, I didn't even stand a chance.

But it's not in my nature to simply turn myself in. Instead, I snarled and kept running. I ran right up the side of the riverbank until it became steep and rocky. Up ahead, I could tell that soon I would have nothing to hold on to and nowhere else to run. Just as the deafening sounds persisted, I searched the area. There didn't seem to be anywhere for me to go but into the water. I looked behind me, back over the area I had just run through. Under the dim light of the moon, I could make out dark forms racing toward me in the distance.

My jaguar lips lifted into a snarl, revealing my canines, until I recognized the dark shadow beasts just ahead of the mist. It was the rest of my unit; they were coming for me. Damian had probably felt my fear through my bond with him and had sent them to help. Relief washed over me at the sight of them. Whatever was happening, we would get through this together.

I turned to face them and darted forward until they collectively make a hard stop. Did they stop, or were they made to stop by something I couldn't see? Behind them I began to make out a massive, inky black mist rolling in. It inched closer with tendrils of shadows as it covered them and continued to tumble in dark, crashing waves in my direction.

What the fuck is that?

I couldn't see them anymore, and I tried not to let it unnerve me. My fellow nagual were among the deadliest Fae in all of Zol Stria, and whoever had sent that particular dark mist would soon learn this was the biggest mistake they had ever made. Those four nagual had become my family, and although I couldn't bear the thought of anything happening to them, I had to have faith that they would fight their way out of whatever it was that had happened. And in that very moment, I knew they would want me to keep running.

But my legs refused to move. I was frozen in place as I considered running in their direction and fighting alongside them in that deep web of darkness. I couldn't imagine losing any of them. Whatever was happening to them, I wanted it to also happen to me. We were a team, and I had to fight for them.

But I had to know what I was up against and, right now, running into what had just consumed them seemed like a suicide mission. Before deciding either way, I scanned the rocks in front of me, but there was no way up. The sound of chaotic darkness thundered in my ears. Instead of turning back I pressed forward, around a bend in the river until I found an opening to a cave. I sensed a familiar presence inside and ran toward him. It was Damian.

"I got here as fast as I could," he said. "I sensed your danger and sent the others to go after you."

I searched his face, and he flashed me his aura. Immediately I sensed genuine concern for me, for himself and the others.

"They've found you. I can teleport us out of here, but we have to go. Now."

Damian was allotted four teleportation spells each year. I had learned from my time in the Academy that the magic of teleportation drew directly from the energy collected during Mercury in retrograde and that the use of teleportation magic had a counter effect on Earth. It messed with technology and communications. In order not to wreak complete havoc on humanity's day-to-day life, each of the shamans were only given four every year by Zol Stria. Damian had saved my life with a teleportation spell the day I first shifted into a jaguar. And he was trying to save me again.

What about the others?

He gave me a confused look. He was the only person who could understand me in my nagual form, and it was only because of our bond.

"What do you mean? What happened to the others?" His eyes searched my jaguar's face for answers, then darted behind me. I guess he expected them to be close behind.

Just then an ear-piercing screech thrummed through the cave, and the dark shadow mist crashed toward us even faster and with more intensity.

"There's no time. Let's go." But before he could chant the teleportation spell, his eyes landed on something immediately behind me. Faster than I could blink, he retracted his aura. His expression darkened with a scowl.

"There you are. Whatever would bring you to this dreadful little hole-in-the-wall?" The voice behind me was deep, controlled and familiar. I had heard it once before, during my transformation ritual.

I couldn't turn my head. My jaguar's body was paralyzed, frozen in place by a force much more powerful than my own. Vast, cold and unyielding power permeated the space around us. My lungs filled with it. The cave walls closed in. Damian's hard glare darted to my jaguar and back at the god who now had me under his command.

Escaping had just become fucking impossible.

CHAPTER 10

How did he find us?

"You don't want to know," the death god said as he walked from behind me to stand between Damian and me in the cave. Every one of his features, except his soft, full lips, were as if carved from stone. His perfectly defined muscles were rock-like structures covered by a sleek designer suit. Straight black hair fell loose and shiny above his shoulders.

Damian shifted on his feet. My jaguar was frozen in place, my connection to her severed. I couldn't feel any of the energy that connected us. She was now only at his command.

He can hear my thoughts?

"Yes, I can," said the god I recognized as Hun-Cane.

In that case, I do want to know. How did you find us?

"Your Grace. The way you must address me is, 'How did you find us, Your Grace?' You know, I blame all of this on what they are teaching you at the Academy. Honestly, this is just unacceptable. Must I be the one to correct you on these simple nuances?"

My apologies. Your Grace, I thought inside the mind of my immovable jaguar's body.

"You see, that wasn't so hard, now was it?" The death god gave me a slight smile, as though he enjoyed all of this control he had. "It's not so much about how I found you, but why I found you. You know, you've got to get better at listening to that little voice inside. Frankly, I'm a little disappointed. But it's for the best, after all. You'll be coming with me so you don't cause any more trouble." His dark eyes shimmered with power.

That little voice. The little voice that didn't trust Trent? Did he give us up? Of course he had. He'd gotten closer to Solana, and she wanted me out of the way. The thought of her and him together felt as though claws raked against my skull. Damian's eyes narrowed to slits.

"*Em chotan*," the death god said, giving an ethereal wave of his hand.

Instantly my jaguar sat down, as still as a statue. I tried to shift back into my human form, but it was no use. There was a mental wall in place between us now, and I could do nothing but bang and scratch against it. This was the god Hun-Cane and he was going to take me back to the Zol Council to lock me up and keep me from becoming whatever it was we had seen in that vision.

"You have caused quite the panic in Zol Stria, young nagual," Hun-Cane said. "I'm here to take you to Xibalba where you will be safe as our ward."

Is that fear for me in Damian's eyes? I felt movement and sensed the presence of others.

"My guards will take you."

I had gone as still as death in that very moment. Both in my body, and now in my mind. I did not want to go to Xibalba.

Your Grace, Great Hun-Cane, please don't punish the others. This was all my fault.

"The nagual are taught to protect each other. To work as a unit. It doesn't surprise me that they chose to help you. In fact, anything else would have gone against your design." His face remained unreadable. I had no idea where he was going with this. "I can sense you are a little... tense." He angled his head, and his eyes concentrated on me.

"Relax, your friends will be fine," he continued. "They are being briefed as we speak, for they are going on a mission to retrieve the relics while you are under our supervision. As soon as we have them all back, you will be free to leave. There are many factors at work here and we must proceed carefully. It really is for the best. The stars have written a path and although confusing, we will watch over you until we know exactly what it is." The god was doing a very poor job of sounding reassuring.

"Take her away," Hun-Cane said, and four Arcana Angels surrounded me.

The Arcana Angels were the deadly protectors of the death gods. Their strength could level buildings and burn holes through monsters and demons. As they approached me, I stopped searching for the tiniest crack in the wall that was blocking me from connecting with my jaguar. It was no use.

The guards wore all-black tactical gear with golden zodiac glyphs decorating their arms. Damian made no effort to resist or fight them off of me. His magic would stand no chance against the power of a god. I was released from the god's paralysis, and I lurched forward, knocking Damian out of the way as I ran.

Ouch! Nails. Nails are piercing my skull. Nails in my brain. My jaguar legs buckled under me, bringing me to the ground as I squirmed in anguish. *Make it stop. Please, please make it fucking stop.*

There's no use running. I will always find you.

The agony inside my skull briefly subsided, and I heard a man scream. I ran back to the death god and his entourage to find Damian on his knees, looking down as blood spilled through his hands that were covering his ears. My jaguar nudged him gently, and he lifted his hands as he met my jaguar's gaze. He grimaced from the pain.

Don't try that again. Hun-Cane's voice reverberated in my mind.

I promise. I won't.

Instantly I was swept away into a dark web of shadows and light, whispers and screams, soft and hard thrusts from the wind. Being teleported by a god was an incredible feeling of being pulled through a tunnel of opposing sensations.

Soon we arrived on the other side of Scorpio Gate. I had never been there before, but I had seen all the Gates in books. Scorpio Gate was built into the side of a massive brown rock located in the arid Mexican desert. The air was dry, crisp and cool because the sun had not yet risen high in the sky. The symbols on the heavy iron gates were in an ancient Mesoamerican language and entirely foreign to me. Yet at the top of the door, carved into the rock, was the familiar Scorpio glyph of the zodiac.

The doors swept open upon our arrival, and the god walked in with his four Arcana Angel guards still surrounding me. I could only follow along. The death god was controlling my jaguar's every movement. *I fucking hate being treated like a caged animal.* The guards on the inside of the gate immediately bowed at his presence, and he gracefully continued along without acknowledging them. The god's jaw was sharp and set, his eyes deep and black. He was magnificent to look at, and once again I felt overwhelmed in his presence. He was the creator of my kind, and of so many other complex things like natural disasters, plague, sickness, famine and death.

I couldn't help but be swept into the awe of the ancient power that vibrated off of him. It was as though I was watching a celestial star in the form of a man. Certainly, this was not like any other creature I'd ever come in contact with, on either side of the Gates of Zol Stria.

We passed through a paved pathway under the harsh desert sun. The death god glowed under its intensity; it was as though he was a reflection of all the rays of light that landed on him. Scattered cacti and tumbleweeds lined the terrain while towering rocks of interesting sizes and formations protruded from the earth. In the distance I saw water, but the closer we got, the further the water became and the more I realized it was just an illusion. We kept going until we reached two large columns at the end of the pathway, and, within just a few feet, there was a beautiful sandstone building.

This was the gateway to other parts of Scorpio Gate. It was quiet and still inside the walls, which felt like a kind of monastery. Several Zol Sen were congregated there, speaking in low voices and peering at large books on tables. A few lifted their heads as we entered, but the older Zol Sen continued doing whatever it was they were doing. Zol Sen were still the most mysterious of all Fae on this side of the Gates, and I had never seen so many together at once. It was said that they lived for thousands of years, and only one Zol Sen was born every decade. They were born with their third eye wide open, and receptive to the multiple dimensions of our universe.

They were the consultants to the rulers of each of the twelve Houses of Zol Stria, and they were the conduits to our connection to the stars. Considered neutral and holy, Master Zol Sen could be either male or female. I gathered there were a few Zol Sen here that were at least that old, although they looked about seventy in human years. They were the ones who didn't look up, their senses so mature and refined after all these years that nothing surprised them. To them, there was nothing they hadn't seen.

There was a cafe to the right where beverages and refreshments were being served. But I knew I wouldn't be offered a cappuccino anytime soon. We headed straight to the back of the building and entered a large doorway with a set of gold-and-red curtains lined with unfamiliar script.

A woman with the cloak of the Zol Sen was waiting for us inside. Her soft blond hair fell loose under her hood, and her crystal-blue eyes were shrouded in mystery. She met our entrance with an alert glance, as though she was expecting us. It was a large space; shelves of books and bottles lined the walls, a desk had books stacked on the sides, and a magnifying glass rested over an ancient atlas that lay open. There was also an exact replica of our planets and our star over by the window, which seemed to have been created to scale, and a huge telescope facing the sky. The most interesting part of the room, however, was the large zodiac wheel engraved into the center of the marble floor.

"Your Grace." She bowed deeply and pressed her hands together in greeting.

He simply gave her a curt nod of acknowledgment. "Go behind those doors," the death god said to me. "You'll find some clothing."

I padded over to where he had gracefully swept his hand, my steps slow and steady. As soon as I entered the small supply closet, I shifted back into my Zol skin. On the otherwise empty shelf in front of me there were a few items of neatly folded clothing. A wave of disappointment washed over me as I saw it, even though I knew there was little hope of finding my battle gear here. Instead, I found an all-white jumpsuit with no pockets. The material was snug and formfitting and it had a Scorpio glyph on the shoulder, along with the symbol for Xibalba on the back. They had also provided white boots with no laces and a pair of socks.

"Zol Zena, we're ready." I heard the death god say to the Zol Sen as I emerged from the small closet.

"Yes, Your Grace."

She reached for a bottle on the wall and removed the one with a sparkly golden substance inside. He took a few elegant steps into the golden zodiac wheel until he reached House Scorpio and, without even a glance in my direction, motioned for me to join him there. Each section of the wheel was so large that at least four people could stand comfortably inside any given section at one time. I had one foot in Sagittarius and the other in Scorpio. Hun-Cane gave me an impatient glare as the Zol Sen poured the golden substance along the perimeter line of the entire circle.

"Stand there, next to me," he commanded.

"Where are we going, exactly?" I studied the large wheel on the floor. These were the wheels of progression; it was how we traveled from one Zodiac House to another once we were already inside of Zol Stria. Hun-Cane cleared his throat. My eyes met his. Oops. "Oh right. Where are we going, *Your Grace?*"

"We are progressing to Xibalba."

A chill rippled down my spine, but not from the cold draft in the room. No, this was from all the stories told of this particular realm of the Underworld.

Only the gods could get to high-security locations within Zol Stria, such as the Underworld known as Xibalba. Hun-Cane and his brother, Vucub-Cane, were the only ones that could transport prisoners to this faction of the Underworld and, of those, only high-profile, extremely dangerous, maximum-security prisoners.

I stood where I was told. Everything was happening so fast; I didn't have time to consider the absolute shit situation I was in. I was going to the Zodiac Prison, and I had no idea for how long.

CHAPTER 11

W e ended up inside another zodiac wheel painted on the ground, and a younger, male Zol Sen looked up at us from an ornate wooden desk just as we arrived.

The death god handed me over to the guards that came in right after us. He returned to the zodiac wheel, his face cold and unreadable as he vanished without another word. The guards surrounded me once again as they escorted me out the double doors of the room and into a dark hallway with golden script lining the tops of the walls. The script characters were of the ancient language of the Zol, and they held magical properties. That could be the reason I couldn't tap into my magic here at all. The hallway was wide and long, with several archways on either side that opened to what looked like a system of caves leading to dark passages.

The smells down here were that of cold earth that had yet to experience the flutter of a light breeze. My feet fell hard on a cool tile floor. I pushed against my awareness in an attempt to scratch at the mind of the jaguar simmering beneath my skin, or to raise a little fire to my fingertips. It was no use. The prison had wards that seemed to lock everything magical about me down. I wondered if that was the same for the Arcana Angels. Was it possible to target only prisoners with the magical security system, or did it work across the board? If that was the case, now that the death god was gone, I had a fighting chance with these guys.

I needed to get out. I wondered if I could I travel back through the zodiac wheel we'd left behind. Could I do it without the death god? Now was my chance to try. As long as I had the element of surprise, I could take on these four guards and make that Zol Sen send me back through to the other side. The Zol Sen weren't known for their fighting skills, that's for sure. If I waited, I could be trapped down here for who knew how long. I would have to take my chances. *Let's see what these guys can do.*

I cracked my neck in preparation for the fight before stopping dead in my tracks. This way no one was behind me, and I could see them move. The guards took four steps forward before they noticed, and I released an exaggerated sigh. I looked down at my hands, which weren't even in restraints. Shame on them for being so confident that I was just going to walk right into this prison.

I wrung my hands together as though I was nervous and then wrapped them around my waist. "My stomach, it hurts so bad. I don't know, it must be something I ate," I whimpered.

The four of them approached me. Before letting them surround me again, I moved fast. Crouching down, I swung my legs, kicking the heels of the guard to my left and throwing him off balance while I delivered a blow to the crotch of the angel on my right. He was half a blink too late on the block, and I immediately registered that speed was on my side. The magical wards hadn't taken that away. The other two guards approached, and I did a quick spin backward so they couldn't close in on me. One of them shot a bolt of electricity at me, but I dodged it with a quick spin to the right and a duck. Now I knew their magic still worked.

I couldn't summon my flames for shit so I had to find another way to get at these fuckers. I couldn't spin forever. I did two flips back, avoiding their blasts again and again. We had learned flips and parkour in Acro Defense Training given that our nagual's innate feline abilities carried over into our Zol skin. I always joked that it should be called ninja class, but, all jokes aside, I loved it. It was one of my favorite courses at the Academy.

My eyes darted behind me, and I only had room for one more backflip. I could take my chances and dart into one of the dark cave-like passageways on my right or left, not knowing where they would lead, or I could stay and get zapped by Mr. Mighty Lightning over there. I dipped into the dark hallway before getting slammed by not just one, not just two, but three forces of Arcana lightning. My legs bolted straight into the dark, menacing cave, but I didn't care as long as I didn't get fried. Just ahead I heard a lot of voices, clamoring and what sounded like the operation of heavy, industrial machines. I hesitated before continuing and slowly stepped into a shadowy crevice of the cave as the footsteps of the angels closed in behind me.

"Come out, little kitty. It's time to show yourself," one of them said.

"That's enough fun for now. Let's not get carried away," another one called out, his voice raspy and dry.

I held my breath, not wanting to give anything away. I had no idea if they had superior senses or not, and I wasn't about to risk it. I stayed deathly still as they got closer. One or two more steps and they would be right in front of me; my obnoxiously bright white jumpsuit would give me away in a heartbeat.

The only way out of this is to fight.

The first two guards walked ahead, not noticing the depth of the crevice I had squeezed myself into. But the guard behind them was more vigilant. He looked straight at me, and I punched him in the nose before he could do a thing.

I followed up by turning and giving him a swift side kick into his stomach, launching his stiff body into the rock behind him, which he hit with a thud.

"Get her!" the one with the raspy voice yelled.

I ducked and tried to run back out the way I came, but the fourth guard had already stepped in my way. I gave him a spinning elbow to the jaw, knocking his face to the side. "Augh!" I heard him grunt as he stumbled. Just then I felt two sharp shocks at my back. A scream left my throat as the pain surged through me, causing my back to arch in agony.

I wanted to fall to my knees, but I fought right through the gripping pain. The second they released the shock I stumbled forward, unable to gain solid footing. Just then another bolt surged around my right wrist, and then I was thrust backward. Again, I refused to fall. I kept my focus on my knees. *Don't buckle.* I yanked at my wrist and dragged my eyes to see what was holding me. It was an electric bolt within a metal clasp that the guard had managed to slap on me. I pulled at it, and it shocked me again.

"We didn't think we would have to do this, since you're one of the death god's little pets. But it looks like you're being a very bad little kitty," said one of the Arcana Angels, his wings rustling just behind him.

All four of them had closed in on me, only inches away. An ache throbbed at my back where they had jolted me, and it was hard to hold myself steady. But I kept my chin high and my shoulders back. They wouldn't know how much they had hurt me.

"Turn around and give us your other hand, kitty," said the freckled angel whose eyes were so small and dark that they reminded me of a bat's.

"Fuck off," I said simply.

Another shock stabbed my left wrist as they locked their electrically charged handcuffs over both hands. They might have a hold on me, but in fighting these four asshats I understood just a little bit more about this place, and that, at least, was a start.

— ◆ —

CHAPTER 12

DAMIAN

For what was probably the first time in my almost ten Zol cycles, I felt completely helpless. With all of my magic and centuries of the manipulation of matter, space and time, there was nothing I could do to prevent Sasha from being captured. It was as though I skipped right past the rage, the anger of losing her and having my abilities restrained, and I fell right into a deep, bothersome darkness that saturated my very soul.

Over these past few years, she had become much more than just another nagual I had to train. She had become my family, and now she was lost, to all of us.

"Hey, what happened?" Zayne asked. He was standing right in front of me, completely naked, but I hadn't heard him walk up.

Jenna, still in her jaguar form, nudged my knee. I lifted my head and blinked at her.

"Where's Sasha? What happened to Sasha? We were told she's 'safe' and that's all," Zayne asked again. His jaw was tight, and his brows were cinched.

Lex and Bjorn, also still in their jaguar forms, stepped in closer.

"She's... She's gone..." I hung my head low.

"Come on," Zayne said. "Let's figure out how to get her back."

I raised my head again, and this time my gaze landed on his outstretched hand. I grasped it in mine. He pulled, and I unsteadily stood, my heart heavy and my head pounding. We walked through the woods in silence. Still loathing myself for letting her get caught, I watched the rest of the unit trek between rocks, bushes and trees as we made our way out of the woods. At least the rest of them hadn't been hurt or captured. I guess this could have been worse. *But they have Sasha, and that is bad enough.*

As we approached the mansion under the cover of night, the lights were still on inside. I stood still and stretched my senses through the wind. I sensed no one in the building.

"Is it safe to go back?" Jenna whispered.

"I'll go first. You guys hang back," I said, walking ahead so they wouldn't have a chance to talk me out of it. As I approached the back door, there was a note taped to it.

This was not me.

Call me.

Trent

I stuffed the note in my pocket and waved at the others not to come forward. I jogged back over to them.

"I'm going to put you under another concealment spell," I said. "It will last about ten minutes, but I swear to Zol that not even a god will find you with it. I'm going in just to get some supplies and we're getting out of here."

They gathered together and I chanted, "*Xitah Ahil*" as I cast out a web of reflection to cover them. It reflected the surrounding environment back out to whoever directed their energy or eyes toward them. I had worked on that spell for years as a hobby, even testing it out on the Wall of Mirrors. It was impossible to find. Over time, the web I was able to cast got larger, but it took time to weave every reflective light together like that. By now it easily covered the entire group with just a little bit extra. Enough to have covered Sasha.

I wish I would have given her this spell before she went racing out of the house. Anger crept in where the darkness was, and I was grateful for it. Anger would motivate me. It would push me to find her. That sad, dark place I went before was crippling. I didn't want to feel that anymore.

I went in and out of the house in minutes, gathering a change of clothing for each of them and the keys to the Land Rover in the garage.

They changed while I concealed the plates and disengaged any trackers on the SUV, making sure to put a powerful deflector spell in place to prevent anyone from tracking this car. Then we drove until we left the state, crossing the Louisiana border into Mississippi, then Montgomery, Alabama.

As I was driving, I pulled out the small paper Trent had left and dialed his number.

He answered on the first ring. "Do you have her?" he said.

"No. Now talk. What do you know?" I hoped he could hear the coldness in my voice. He had blown my trust. The rest of the unit was listening in, and I could sense Zayne tensing next to me.

"Look, it wasn't me. I hope you know that." Trent's voice was firm, convincing.

Jenna snarled from the back seat.

I, however, did not keep my voice calm. "Then how the fuck did they find us?"

"I don't know. But I know you're going to try and get her back. If you get word to her, please tell her that I love her. That I did *not* betray her."

I hung up the line. He had no new information for me, so this conversation was pointless.

"There's no sense in hiding from the gods," Jenna said. "She ran out of that house like a bat out of hell when he admitted he was having an affair with Solana. She might as well have had sirens on her head. I bet she didn't have the mind to keep up her deflector spell. All the death god had to do was track her energy. So, as far as I'm concerned, this is all Trent's fault."

"Now the question is, do we go after Sasha, or go after the relics?" Bjorn asked as he scratched at his beard.

"Hun-Cane wants us to continue on with our original mission. By taking her and not us, he doesn't have to take any risks with Sasha. There is a prophecy of the Zol-bound mate, and in that vision, she looked like she was mated to the UnZol King. I'm guessing the king needs her to make his rebirth complete," I said.

"If the death god is so powerful, why can't he just go and get those relics back himself? Why does he even need us?" Jenna asked this simple question, but I knew she was asking out of frustration, not because she didn't know the answer.

"The death god can put people in Xibalba, and they can control us, their warriors," Lex said. "But that's it. We are the twin gods' elite force, the extension of their power in Zol Stria and the mortal world. That's why he and his brother created us. To go and do things like retrieve relics and fight monsters. This is why we have the powers we have. You know this. It was in our Creator Origins class two semesters ago," he said, chiding her lightly.

"Yeah, that's right. I remember. So, let's go get those relics back and get Sasha the fuck out of there. They better not hurt her." Jenna crossed her arms in front of her chest. "Do you believe Trent?"

"Fuck no. Trent is the very reason she's in that shithole Xibalba. But we can't get to the relics now, not without ese pendejo," I said, and everyone fell silent.

"So you think busting her out of a high-security prison is a better choice?" Lex asked, skepticism lacing his voice.

Just then I decided where it was we were going. I released my grip on the steering wheel, easing back into the seat to settle in for the long drive ahead. There was only one witch I could trust to help us, and we could be there in just a few hours.

"Yes, actually I do," I answered him. "When you've lived as long as I have, you hear the stories. Even if no one has ever escaped the prison, I've met a few former guards in Zol Stria. I remember when one had a nervous breakdown inside, after being down there with the damned way too long and not having the right personality type for that kind of work. They brought him to a healer, but it was no use; he lost it. He raged out on a crowd of people at a winter solstice party at the Zol Temple of Aquarius. He brutally attacked about twenty of them, killing half a dozen. Other, more coherent guards that were forced to retire early said it was fifty times worse than any of the other Underworld prisons. Makes them seem like a theme park in comparison."

"That's not making me feel better," Jenna said.

"Sasha's tough, baby. She's going to be all right." Lex's tone was soft and soothing. I barely heard him since his words were meant for Jenna.

"Lex is right. She can handle the prison and a lot more." I was telling myself as much as I was telling them.

An hour later I drove off the highway and past strip malls. Past streetlights, trailer parks and shacks, through a barely lit side road in the backcountry. A place many others would avoid at this time of night. This was what they called the boondocks.

Zayne had kept me company most of the drive, which helped to keep my mind distracted from what exactly was happening to Sasha. I'd bet whatever it was, she wasn't making it easy for them. But now Zayne was passed out in the passenger seat much like the others in the back. My headlights were the only thing illuminating the narrow backroad we were on.

Let's see, Gaelle's place should be right up here. Her rustic brown mailbox came into view, and I was relieved to see it hadn't changed. I made a right turn up the long, gravel driveway that appeared to lead nowhere until I reached a wooden house at the edge of a lake. I turned off the car.

The porch light turned on, and Gaelle opened the front door, just as beautiful as I remembered.

CHAPTER 13

SASHA

We continued down the long, barely paved pathway. When we entered the processing unit, there was a Zol Troll staring at security monitors who didn't even look up as we arrived. A ghostly white Fae sat at the reception desk. The desks were made of intricately carved wood, and they were lined with the ancient Zol language of the stars. I imagined they were invoking every manner of security ward.

The Arcana Angel with bat eyes said, "She's ready for the Drop."

I hadn't heard the term before, but I guessed it wasn't good.

A pale, blue-haired Fae with thin, round glasses and long limbs retrieved a rectangular obsidian stone from the desk drawer. "Open your hand." He eyed the stone then my arm, which I'd kept at my back.

Bat Eyes said, "Give me the stone," and he snatched it up from the desk then stood behind me.

I kept my hand balled into a fist.

"Open your hand," he grunted impatiently.

"Say please," I purred.

"Open your fucking hand." He sounded like he was about to lose it and punch me again.

My lips curled into a smirk. "You need to learn how to talk to a lady." I opened my hand, and he pressed the cool stone against my palm, which was strapped to my back.

"She's all yours," Bat Eyes said to a seven-foot-tall prison officer who had appeared in the hallway behind the reception desk. This was the Zol Wolf who would escort me to my cell, which was deep underground.

"So, you're a nagual and a fire elemental." He read this off the obsidian stone given to him by the blue-haired Fae. "Your magic or abilities don't work in here, so don't even try. Because you're now classified as a flight risk, you'll be held in isolation until we can see some good behavior out of you."

He dragged his gaze up and down my body, and I caught a lustful glimmer in his eye. The muscled wolf led me to an elevator at the center of the room that dropped down an open circle. I shot my eyes down, seeing floor after floor of prison cells, leading what seemed like infinitely downward into a murky black void.

So far, we had passed four floors as we dropped down in the old metal elevator.

"Is this why they call it the Drop? Because we go down so far?" I asked.

He gave me a cold stare out of the corner of his eye. Then he dragged his glare to my chest and let it linger there for a moment too long. He turned to face me and took several paces forward, until I could feel his heated breath on my face. "Something like that," he mumbled, and I glared back at him.

We dropped another five floors down while he just stood there, trying to intimidate me. The farther we dropped, the more it smelled like cold, wet earth mixed with metal and soot.

My hands were still bound by the electrical handcuffs that probably had some sort of magic suppression within them. I debated either headbutting him or shoving my shoulder into his chest, but neither seemed like a good choice within the tight space. I had counted sixteen floors when the elevator finally clunked to a stop.

The Zol Wolf kept staring at me, until he angled his head to the side so his lips were next to my jaw. A heartbeat later I felt his soggy, thick tongue flat against my skin as he raked it up to my cheek. Right before he lifted off, I whipped my face around and caught his tongue in my teeth. I clamped down until I tasted his blood, and he released an angry moan while slamming me backward into the elevator wall, breaking himself free from my bite. My lips curled upward into a smirk as he reached for his tongue, his brows cinched as a growl left his throat.

"You crazy bitch," he mumbled with a wounded tongue. Some of his blood was splattered on my white jumpsuit. I spit blood on the floor as pain surged down my back. It would be sore for a while after this.

"Stop complaining. You'll heal within the hour, and I'll have such a lovely memory of our time together," I hissed.

He grabbed my shirt with one hand, holding me in place while he smacked me with the back of his other hand. It stung, but I didn't flinch. I slowly returned my eyes to lock with his in an unyielding gaze.

"Now, we're even," he said. "Why don't you start to play nice? It will make your time here so much more pleasant."

"After what I did to your tongue, you can imagine what I'd do to your dick." I threw my head back and laughed madly.

He reached down and adjusted himself before giving me a smirk of his own, wetting his lips. "Get moving," he grunted. I walked ahead, and he followed close behind me.

As I walked down the long hallway lined with several doors, it was very quiet. Very still. Almost as though this wasn't the dark world of death that I'd envisioned in my mind, where trials would be fought for your life. What was behind the five iron doors I had passed on the way here? My senses had been turned off, as though I was never of the realm of magic.

As we approached the cell, he said in a gritty voice, "They had you assigned to a bigger cell down the hall, but I think you're better suited for this one." He released a dark chuckle, and I slowly stepped forward.

The room was small and smelled of death. The walls were as if carved from the side of a mountain, with white paint slapped over uneven stone. There was a cot. No blankets or pillow. A tiny stainless-steel toilet and sink were next to the bed. Just as I was turning around in my tight cell, a flesh rat scurried over my feet and squeezed itself into a small hole in the corner. Flesh rats would prefer to eat only raw meat. They were scavengers found all over Zol Stria and had grown to be a nuisance after feeding on the dead carcasses during the Faellen Wars.

This place is worse than I thought. Disgusting.

"Make yourself at home, little kitty. You'll be lucky if you get out of here any time in the next decade. You'll be begging for my dick by the next time I visit." He grabbed himself again and I rolled my eyes.

"Nunca en mi vida, pendejo," I said. *Never in my life, asshole.*

He stepped toward me, closing the gap between us, and I expected him to lash out again. Maybe this time with his elemental magic, which I guessed was fire from the golden embers I saw in his eyes whenever I pissed him off. But just then his radio sounded.

"Cirrus, we have an issue in gen pop."

Never breaking his stare, he pressed the button on the radio and answered, "I'll be right there." He backed out of the cell and locked the door shut. "We'll continue this conversation later," he shouted, moving quickly down the hall.

At the other end of the cell was a small glass window in a thick, steel frame. I did not expect to see a picturesque garden with narcissus and night-blooming jasmine through the glass. It was a breathtaking scene out of an ideal vacation. I scanned the room for hallucination spells, but I couldn't find any. It didn't mean there weren't any, it just meant my ability to sense them was being stifled by the magical security system. After pacing about for a while, I sat in the center of the floor, facing the window. I crossed my legs, just as I had done so many times before. It was time to go into my mind.

After years of practice, I had become very adept at entering the meditative state. Where it used to take up to five minutes to reach those confused crevices of my internal world, now I saturated every part of my being the moment I closed my eyes. There was no need to go to my zen goat shed or lap around the lake in my aunt's house in Villalba. Now, I was instantly exactly where I wanted to be, searching for the layers of security, illusion and magic keeping me here.

Where is the truth?

Where my magic couldn't go, my mind would travel. I focused in on Damian, since he was the last person I had seen and I wanted to track him. I could follow our bond just about anywhere, and yet down here it was impossible. Over the years at the Academy, I had captured the energy markers of the entire unit, and, after trying to track them, I learned that was impossible as well. The wards here were too strong.

In here, all I had was time. I would keep trying until I found the slightest crack in the magical wards. All I needed was a little sign of weakness.

After trying for a while, I slowly opened my eyes. My gaze drifted to the window, but I had to stand to look out of it. I came to my feet and stared out of the expansive window to the beautiful view outside. I couldn't put my finger on it, but something was off about this view. Digging deep, I found some energy reserves and extended my presence outside the window to the surrounding lush veranda. My awareness slipped through the wards in a million different misty pieces. I began to wrench and yank at the folds of images before me, scanning them for some break in pattern, for the slightest inconsistency. I almost decided that this was real, before I realized that this was an incredibly well-crafted hallucination spell. At the very ends of the scene outside my window there was the faintest inconsistency in the colors of the flowers.

I pulled at it until the edges of the illusion lifted.

So many lies. This is just another one.

Just as I found the spell's vulnerability, the lush landscape of bushes and flowers began to disintegrate to reveal miles of sooty, black, rocky underground terrain. Odd black roots and vines curled around black-and-grey rocks through the hilly terrain. Thousands of workers pulled at carts, coughing under clouds of ash and smoke, being supervised by eight-foot-tall trolls, vampires and minotaurs that wore metal vests and bore large wands that crackled with electricity. One Fae with blue-and-gold wings, olive skin and blue hair fell as he carried a bucket of rocks that had been mined. Immediately the troll came to him with his crackling wand and shocked him with bright blue electricity. The Fae writhed on the ground in pain. When the troll stopped zapping him, he struggled to stand.

Xibalba was a place for the worst souls. Murderers, rapists, terrorists, high-level thieves and those who enjoyed torturing others for fun. Many of these also happened to be the Dark Zodiac, those who opposed everything that Zol Stria stood for and looked to the UnZol King as their rightful leader.

Those were the people I saw through the window. The workers, both male and female, outside in soot-covered white jumpers just like mine, hauled heaps of rock from one part of the desolate Underworld to another. Maybe when they released me from isolation, I would end up right next to them, another body among the masses of those imprisoned here.

Why would they even bother to hide this part of it from me? Did they want me to discover what was behind it? Or did I find a weakness in their magical infrastructure?

If I could find this crack in their magic, maybe I would find another.

CHAPTER 14

SASHA

T he days began to blend together, and after the sixth day confined to this dingy little cell, my energy had been completely depleted. There was something about this place, the darkness and the fear that fueled my power, which was missing in its entirety. I thought the Underworld would be a spectacle of darkness. That here there would be plenty of dark energy for me to tap into. And if I couldn't use the dark energy for my powers, at least I could channel my awareness outside of these four walls. But that wasn't happening. I hadn't been able to go anywhere at all in any of my meditations.

Lunch appeared on the floor by the front door as it usually did, and I just stared at it. Although, there wasn't much to stare at. White bread with some kind of synthetic lunch meat and an apple. After some time, the flesh rat peeked its head out of the little hole.

"I bet you're wondering if I'm going to eat that. Well, I'm not. Help yourself." I waved at the tiny creature as it considered launching itself at the tasty meal. I guessed it must have been hungry to be considering my sandwich. For now, it decided not to risk it and went back into hiding.

My hair felt itchy against my scalp, probably because I hadn't washed it in a week, and my body began to smell in ways that I wasn't at all comfortable with. I was dying for a shower.

At dinnertime, the plain sandwich was replaced by a slice of some kind of meat that I couldn't identify and white mush that hinted at being very watery mashed potatoes. Despite my hunger, I also didn't touch the dinner. At this point, I had no plan behind the not eating. I was just really sick of the food and so utterly drained of my sense of self. Feeling only emptiness where my power had been wearing on me.

I was alone all day, all night, with no communication with the outside world, and I needed to know what was going on. For days I banged on the door. The windows. I screamed.

A few more days passed and finally, as I was sitting in a meditative position on the floor I heard shuffling just outside the door.

"Hey little kitty," I heard Cirrus purr as he opened the door behind me. "I told you I'd come back to visit. Did you miss me?"

My eyes fluttered open and I let him take two steps inside the cell as I listened but didn't hear any other footsteps. The moment I realized he was alone I turned around and lunged for him with all my strength. After I knocked him down, I ran down the corridor, looking for an escape.

"You don't want to do that," the guard snarled. His voice was raspy, matching his gruff appearance.

Oh yes, I do.

None of the doors would open. My eyes darted back to him. He was up on his knees, reaching for his holster. He pulled a wand out and shot the electricity at me. I dodged it before it could land, turned back around, and ran toward him. I lunged at him again, slamming myself into him with much less strength then I was used to, this time dodging the electric wand at my right, then my left as he directed it with more intensity. I bit down on my bottom lip and lurched, just as I would have done in my jaguar form. He took a swing at me, and I ducked, punching him in his ribs on my way down. He swung again and again, landing a fist to my jaw as my head snapped to the right. *Dig deep Sasha, you've got to dig deep.* I pictured my unit, the Fae that had become my family. I needed to get back to them. I had to find strength from within.

I jumped to the right in time to avoid a zap from his wand and pivoted fast enough to land my fist to his nose, the sound of crunching bones a sweet reward. The moment he stumbled backward I put my foot in place behind him, knocking the two-hundred-pound prison guard to the ground with a loud thump.

I pounced on him, pressing my knees into his shoulders and pinning him to the ground. That's when I lowered my head and took in a long, deep sniff. His eyes glowed amber with rage and I caught a whiff of his anger. It was slight, subtle and hidden by some kind of ward that I couldn't recognize, but it was enough. I pulled at that morsel of emotion. His anger was just a manifestation of fear, and fear was powerful fuel for a nagual. I needed it to soak into me, to replenish my energy which had been so empty, to feed my soul and my sanity. Being locked away in that dreadful room without access to the energy I needed was its own form of slow, painful torture.

I latched on to the tendrils of shadow that he emitted, and once he realized what I was doing, he tried to pull it back, but I had already had too tight a grip. His fear was mine, and I wasn't letting go. I punched him on his cheek, my knuckles ringing from the impact. But not hard enough to knock him out.

I needed him to be awake and continue to fear me so I could soak in more. *So hungry.*

My eyes rolled to the back of my head with the rich satisfaction of replenishing my energy. In a heartbeat he snapped his wrist free of my grasp and clamped his palm around my breast. I glared at him as his eyes glowered at me and his fingers squeezed against my skin. I tapped into that dark energy to fight his hand back. I had found the beginnings of my strength from sourcing his darkness and it was all I needed to overpower him. Calmly, I said to the gruff Fae underneath me, "How do I get out of here?"

"You don't," he grumbled as he resisted my restraint.

"We could do this all day." I drove my knees hard into his shoulder as I got closer and sucked in the irritation that spilled unwillingly out of him. Hard to keep your emotions in check when you were getting assaulted. "Now, tell me exactly... how do I get out of here?" I asked while tilting my head to the side.

"Like he said, you don't." I heard a familiar majestic voice from behind. It was the voice of my creator.

With my hands still pressing on the guard's wrists, I turned my head to find the other twin god of death, Vucub-Cane, standing behind me. The opposite of his brother, this death god had thick white hair and grey eyes, which were a stark contrast to his golden skin. As I watched him gracefully approach us, I hungrily sucked in the guard's fear, because he certainly was nervous to have been caught in such a predicament, unable to control his prisoner. It may have been the last use of my own free will while in the presence of the death god, so I had to make it count.

Vucub-Cane simply sauntered gracefully into my cell and positioned himself in front of the window. I could still see him from the hallway. "Come on, let him go. You've had your fun. You and I need to talk." His voice was smooth and cool, as though this was just another average day.

I looked down at the guard who had finally given up fighting against me. I let him go, and, as I lifted off of him, he rushed to his feet and snatched electrical handcuffs from his side. I gave him my hands, and he slapped them on me, the charge stinging my skin.

"Take those off. She doesn't need them," the death god said, still looking out the window.

Cirrus hesitated, then released me from his grip, and I took the chance to give him a sly smirk. He retracted his aura tightly around him now, not releasing even the slightest sliver for me to feed off. Too bad. The death god couldn't put me into a state of paralysis in my Zol skin, at least that much I knew. But I also knew that this was his domain. He could probably send dozens of guards in here if he wanted to, and I wouldn't stand a chance against them.

I lifted my chin and entered the cell with my shoulders back, curious now about what it was he wanted with me.

"You've caused quite a stir in Zol Stria. The Council has been meeting at House Leo, deliberating on the meaning of the vision." He wouldn't turn to look at me, and I knew I would grow bored of listening to him while only looking at his back.

"And what did they come up with, Your Grace?" I asked casually. I had wracked my brain about this, and I still couldn't figure out what I was doing with the UnZol King in that vision.

Now the death god turned to face me, subtly pulling at the edges of his jacket. More as a thing to do with his hands than for any other reason I could imagine, because his white satin suit was impeccable. "No need for the formalities." He took me in briefly and shifted his gaze around the small cell of mine. "They didn't come up with anything, but I did. You are the reincarnation of the UnZol King's mate. She was the first nagual, and you share her DNA. He is coming back for you, as his mate."

My skin prickled under the surface as my jaguar stirred at those words.

"He must have you, and the relics, to return."

I shuddered at the thought of being mated to the most wickedly evil motherfucker to have ever lived in all of Zol Stria. *Why would the stars choose this path for me?* "How do you know this?" I asked, doing my best to keep anger from filling my voice.

"Because I was the one who made sure you had her DNA." He moved to face me as I peered at him. "You and your unit figured out that it wasn't the Dark Zodiac that had killed Lily, it was Ixia. One of the Zol Stria Council members. She sure has a vengeful side, doesn't she? And she sure hated your aunt. She killed her just because Damian fell in love with her. Shameful." There was very little emotion, if any, in his voice, yet I did pick up the slightest teasing glimmer in his eye.

"Yet as vengeful as she is, Ixia is one of the most astute members of the Council. Her contributions to Zol Stria are countless, making her one of the richest and most powerful Council members of the twelve Houses. And she was on to something. Right under the Council's noses, she had her own people working out the calculations of the nagual's birth dates with her advanced prisms and contraptions. Right before you were born, she suspected that you could be the one born with the perfect timing, and star alignment, to be a match for the UnZol King, just as I had intended." He explained this as though it was some retelling of a movie he had just seen and not my fucking life he was talking about.

"Instead of involving the Council, she decided to go after you all on her own because of your connection to Damian. And she came up with the perfect plan to satisfy her thirst for revenge. She decided that the best course of action, for Zol Stria and herself, was to kill Lily."

"She knew Damian well enough to know it would break him. Everybody knows that no one survives those maddening mind games the shadows play right before a nagual's transformation without their guide or shaman. And, my dear, after her death you were without both."

Just then I caught a flicker of admiration that flashed in his eyes, then it was gone.

"As you know, after Lily died, he disappeared. By the time Ixia saw him again, she had new hope for them. There was just one tiny detail her clever mind overlooked, and it was because of her arrogance. She underestimated you. She wasn't counting on you figuring out how to cross the Gates all on your own to track down your shaman. You really threw a wrench in her plans."

My jaw began to ache from how long I had been clenching it.

"She was going to reveal her victory at the ritual and take all the glory, but with you alive, she couldn't. She patiently hunted you in the background, until she decided to strike in Miami and got closer to Damian just so she could understand you better. But yet again, she underestimated you."

I never shifted my gaze from him. Didn't blink once as he told me the story. My training had taught me to suppress emotions because here, in Zol Stria, your emotions made you prey.

"Right now, she's vying for her old position. As I speak, she's working to convince everyone, with evidence, that you are the UnZol King's mate and so a direct threat to Zol Stria. And now, because of the vision, she's been able to justify herself so well to the Council that they are likely going to grant her old position back."

"And that's exactly what you want them to do," I breathed, the words tumbling out.

He met my glare. "I certainly do."

I wondered how much more he would be willing to reveal to me. Thoughts raced at the back of my mind. Why would this god of death want the UnZol King back? What did it mean for me to be the mate of the UnZol King? What could I do to break the mating bond? I wondered many things, and I expected the death god to have all of these answers. I opened and closed my hands to keep from clawing at the insides of my palms.

"You ask many questions of me, nagual, and I'm not inclined to share answers unless telling you will somehow serve me. Lest you forget, I am the god of death. My brother and I oversee the Underworld. We aren't the gods of the sea or the sun, balance or justice, equity, plants, love or any other noble worldly cause. No, we are the gods of fear and destruction. Of humiliation and defeat. So, if you are looking for some comfort, do not look to me." He searched my eyes.

"Let go of what you thought you knew," he said. "You thought you knew love because of Trent? You thought that he was your 'person?' That kind of love got exposed in the wilderness with no wards to protect you. When you mate with the UnZol King, you will be the Queen of the Zodiac. The queen of all queens. There will be no one and nothing that can stop you. That is the power everyone is so afraid of you having. That is the power you yourself are afraid of having."

"Why are you doing this?" My brows pinched together. Until now he had been very still, like a statue. I couldn't read one shred of emotion in his body or face, except for what he wanted me to see. Yet with this single question, his eyes shifted to the left and his hands moved to his pockets. It was as though he was considering answering me.

"You still don't understand? Gods are patient. We are indefinite and we have time. I planted the seeds, now it's time for me to watch them grow."

That wasn't an answer.

"Enough talk. You will find out soon enough, I suppose." He left the room and closed the door. Fear of what was to come tried to wash over me, but I pushed it aside. Now was not the time to be afraid. It was time to fight.

CHAPTER 15

DAMIAN

Five Days Earlier

The smell of cedar filled my lungs, followed by hibiscus and citrus. Although this place looked like it was falling apart on the outside, it was the picture of modern comfort on the inside. The open floor plan was well decorated, with a combination of eclectic and contemporary furniture and decor. The living room, dining room and kitchen was one large space, while off to the right there was an open door leading to Gaelle's work area, where bottles and books were labeled and carefully placed on shelves among fresh herbs.

Gaelle held the steaming cup of hibiscus tea out toward me.

"I need something stronger," I grunted.

"I'll take it," Jenna said, and Gaelle gave her a soft smile as she handed her the cup. "Thank you." Jenna held the cup just under her nose and took in a deep inhale.

Lex and Zayne remained in the back by the door as Bjorn made his way around the room, scanning for wards.

"I've got just the thing for you." Gaelle returned to the kitchen and began opening and closing cabinets. The long, black strands of her hair fell loosely around her brown-and-yellow printed dress. Seashell and thread bracelets covered her right wrist and similar necklaces hung from her neck. Her golden-brown skin was smooth and bright.

"It's ok, guys, really. She's one of us," I insisted as Gaelle went on preparing something in the kitchen. Yet as I said this, even I couldn't relax after all we'd been through.

Lex made his way to the large beige couch as the others sat in the armchairs around the living room.

"You haven't changed at all since I last saw you," I said as I approached Gaelle in the kitchen.

"Oh, well, you know being the weird witch in the woods has been good to me." She handed me a short glass with what looked like liquid gold over ice. "Anyone else want one?"

"Sure."

"Yeah."

"Would love it," came from the others.

As she turned around to get other glasses from the cabinet, I cast a spell neutralizer over the liquid just in case. One could never be too careful. I took a sip, the froth at the top tickling a little when it met my lips. "Oh, whisky sour, I should have known." I gave her a soft smile, and she returned a quick wink.

When she was done serving us, we took our seats on the couch, her thigh making contact with mine as she sat at an angle to face us.

"So great that you guys came by like this," she said. "I don't particularly like having visitors. Which is why I moved out here all those years ago. But Damian, and of course his friends, are always welcome here." Her bright smile revealed her perfectly straight white teeth. She spoke with a light French accent that was soft and welcoming.

"Thank you, Gaelle. We won't be staying long. We just need some help, and you're the only one I know that has ever gotten into Xibalba."

Her eyebrows cinched, and the warm smile was wiped from her face. "Oh no, no. You're not asking me to do that." She stood up and began pacing the room.

"Yes. I am. A friend of ours is there and we need to get her out." I remained sitting and took a long sip of the drink. Maybe if I had another, I could make this conversation go easier.

"In case you haven't noticed, we are nagual. We can handle the dark planes. We live in them," Jenna said reassuringly. She quickly removed her clothing and shifted, pulling in the dark tendrils all around her to emphasize her point.

Gaelle merely looked at her as she continued to pace the room nervously. "Damian. Why do you bring this to me? I don't think it's a good idea. I don't care how important you think your friend is. This is a trap." She shook her head.

Gaelle was always a bit odd, to say the least. She was eclectic, artistic and creative, and in all the hundreds of years I had known her she was always honest. Just then, I noticed a small movement in the corner. It was as though a small creature, like a cat, had skittered across the floor. Its long tail was still visible from behind Lex's chair, and I had my eyes fixed on it. Lex turned, following my gaze.

"Oh, that's just Lefou. He's harmless. I brought him here with me after my last visit to House Leo." She bent to her knees and called it over to her.

Lefou leapt into her arms. His fingers and face were a bright blue, while the hair that covered him was entirely white. His eyes were a deeper blue, like the ocean, and he simply stared at us, his ears twitching slightly. Zol Monkeys, like many of the animals in Zol Stria, possessed a singular magical ability that they honed over centuries. These creatures could cast short reflection spells, making themselves invisible for brief periods of time. They weren't known for being aggressive, because they relied on their ability to hide for their survival.

"We are well aware that it could all be a trap, and we don't care. We need you to help us with our Descent so we can do whatever it is we need to do to get her out of there," Zayne said.

Gaelle took a moment to glance at each of the unit's faces. Her eyes locked with each of theirs for a handful of heartbeats. "You're sure you all want to do this? Once you go in, there's no guarantee you'll make the Climb to come back out." Her voice was shaky, her eyes wide with fear as she spoke.

"We're sure," Zayne said as the others nodded and glared back at her, in agreement.

"Fine. Fine, you want to go down there and kill yourselves?" She threw her hands up and paced in a circle. "I will help you. I must... help you. Damian, I told you I owed you and I keep my promises."

"Thank you. You do owe me." I released a sigh, grateful she was going to keep her word.

"Now I'm curious, what did he do? To think after all this time, I thought Damian was born without a Zol," Zayne said, chuckling.

"I was a Dark Mage in Zol Stria, hundreds of moons ago," Gaelle began. "The Vicar of House Pisces had made our family their slaves after the Faellen Wars, and I was to serve their House for eternity as punishment for my grandparents' rebellion. Damian helped me escape after he brought the Pisces nagual to his post." There was a distinct glimmer in her eyes from the memory, and I remembered our many nights together here in a much smaller, less comfortable version of this very cottage after I had helped her find her freedom.

"So, I see that you two have a history," Jenna joked as the right side of her mouth curled.

"Yes, you could say that." I approached Gaelle and placed my hand on her shoulder. "I will never ask you for another favor after this. We need your help."

She stared back at me with her dark ebony eyes. "I wish you would reconsider. But fine. I am a woman of my word. Let's get started."

Chapter 16

Sasha

After several days locked up in this room with nothing to do except go over every bit of my conversation with the death god Vucub-Cane, time felt like it was pressing in on me. In just two weeks Pluto would arrive, and it would be the closest that Pluto had been to our planet in hundreds of years, and this was when they would bring back the UnZol King. Yet, I was locked up in this bottomless pit of an Underworld unable to do jack shit about it.

So, I let my mind work out some things. I thought of the death god and considered his connections and relationship with the Zol Council. It had begun to dawn on me that Vucub-Cane had access to the Obsidian Heart, the Snake Tongue, the Blood Ruby and the Stone Mind, which were the relics the Council had in security. And by working with Solana and the Dark Zodiac, he could then get the ones she had, and finally with me, he would have everything needed to complete the rebirth of the UnZol King by the return of Pluto. He was hiding this from his brother, Hun-Cane, who was working with the Zol Council and who was the one who had locked me up in the first place.

I tried everything to track Damian and the others to let them know what I had figured out, but whenever I reached for them I came up against a huge, black mental wall. There was a barrier in place to prevent me from communicating with them. It must have been Vucub-Cane's doing. He was the only one with the power to block me. Sitting on my cot, I curled my knees further into my chest and wrapped my arms around them.

I heard a knock on the door, and I simply stared at the doorknob, wondering if that was a real knock or a knock I had imagined. A handful of heartbeats later the door opened wide. The same four Arcana guards who had brought to this cell now approached me.

"Oh, look who's here. Has it been fun in isolation?" asked Bat Eyes as soon as he opened the door.

"It's been a blast. I've even made a friend." I wasn't being entirely sarcastic. The flesh rat and I had begun to get close over the past few days. He nibbled on the small parcels of mystery meat I threw him while I whined about how miserable I was in here. It would be fair to say we'd started to form a small but significant bond.

"Get up. You're coming with us," he growled.

I considered putting up a fight and taking out the four of them. Like the last time, it wouldn't be without a few scratches, but it might be worth my time. But my hands felt empty, as did my chest. I didn't think I had it in me.

"Where are we going?" I rose to my feet, my shoulders slumped while my eyes passively scanned the guards up and down. I had been in here for six days without a shower, my magic suppressed, and my intense hunger for dark energy growing by the minute. I trotted over to Bat Eyes, cocking my head to the side in a nervous twitch and scratching my matted hair. The look on their faces seemed satisfied. As though they were happy to see me broken. That one thought was all I needed to light the tiniest fire in my soul.

Instead of waiting for him to answer my question, I pulled my hand back faster than I'd expected, relieved I had managed to conjure up some speed. I landed my fist with a crack against his rock-solid jaw and felt the reverberation of the impact in my knuckles as I studied him carefully for the slightest hint of the shadows.

Oh my Zol, please be angry with me. Please be pissed that I just did that.

And there it was, a tiny sliver of dark energy swirling at his collar. A break in his retracted energy that I sucked up, savoring every tiny fragment of it. I kept pulling it into me as he rubbed his jaw. Dark energy from an Arcana Angel was more potent than any other dark energy I had ever tasted. Even when the other guards grabbed me by the arms and restrained me, I hungrily drank from the shock and anger Bat Eyes directed toward me.

"More," I yelled out as I thrashed and kicked when they grabbed me. I was so thirsty for the taste of the dark shadow mist. I was nothing without it. One of my kicks landed in the gut of a second guard, who released another sliver, and I fed off of his dark emotions immediately. I just wanted more. I fought them until an electric charge shocked me from behind as one of the guards managed to snap those wretched electrical handcuffs on both my wrists.

"That's enough. One more outburst and we'll cover you in a Zol charge so strong you'll go unconscious. Then all we'll have to do is carry you out," the shifty guard said.

I snarled at the four of them. "Fine. Fine. I'll go," I conceded, and they led me out of the room.

We made our way through a series of high walkways, where down below I saw every kind of prisoner working at mechanical equipment. Huge, tattooed Fae beasts lifted large metal sheets as the worker Fae, male and female, bound them together in pressing machines. They were making military gear. As I peered down at them, one of the guards said to the other, "They should have put her down there, with gen pop. See how tough she is then."

I nearly jumped over the rail to get down there. I could see the dark energy swirling around them. Could almost taste it from all the way up here. But it was too far to pull, and we were walking too fast for me to get ahold of any. I stopped walking and gripped the steel rail on the walkway, my knuckles turning white from the tightness of my hold. In the few heartbeats that I stood there, I greedily called to the shadows. I soaked in every inky black mist and shadowy tendril in my radius. The tiny bit I could find thrummed through my skin and right into my center.

It made me realize that the cell I was imprisoned in was designed for dark-energy-feeding Fae like me. It kept us confined, while depriving us of the one thing we liked better than sex: the very dark energy that fed our existence. Those prison cells robbed us of our strength, making us weak and desperate. I sure as shit hoped I was never going back to that cell.

They proceeded to walk me out of two large iron gates as we continued on down a long passageway surrounded by odd-looking trees and narcissus flowers until we reached a beautiful, sprawling Spanish-style hacienda. It was right at the large entrance to the magnificent hacienda that the energy shifted. It was bright here, where everywhere else in the Underworld seemed dull and subdued.

This was Vucub-Cane's palace, and it looked exactly as it did in the Zol history books.

CHAPTER 17

DAMIAN

We decided that tomorrow, during the black moon, would be the best time to take our leap to the other side. After showering and freshening up, everyone found a comfortable place to sleep for the night, except me. I was outside on the wooden back patio, sitting and watching the breeze swish the leaves of the oak trees that grew just a few feet away while the sound of crickets and frogs rang out in the dark night.

"Everyone's settled in." Gaelle gently placed her soft hands on my shoulders. I placed a hand on top of hers. "Why are you doing this?" she asked. "Why are all of you risking being damned to an eternity in the Underworld for a nagual?"

She sat in the wooden patio chair next to me, and I began to explain the long road had that brought us here, starting with the death of Lily to the vision from the Cihuatl.

"I see," she said softly as she gently swept her hand along Lefou's tail. "You really loved Lily. I remember you coming by and telling me all about her. You broke my heart then. Just like you've broken so many hearts over the years."

"I never wanted to hurt you, or anyone. My heart is a fickle thing. It speaks only in riddles and so far, Lily has been the only woman who has been able to solve them." My eyes narrowed on Gaelle as she stood before me, the moonlight casting a soft glow around her.

"My heart speaks in riddles, too. But I found someone who loved me, unconditionally. He was sweet and kind. But he was human, and he died several years ago. We had three children. They've grown and moved away, but I visit with them from time to time. They know what I am, as my daughters have some slight abilities of their own. But for the grandchildren, I alter my appearance to show wrinkles whenever I see them. They are too young to understand. I've cast strong reflection spells on all of them, so the Council can't find their magic. Lefou has helped me a lot with that."

I chuckled. "It sounds like you found happiness."

"I did. It was marvelous, and I know that when the time is right, I will find love again. But I do get lonely, once in a while."

My eyes shifted from the dark woods to meet her stare, then my eyes drifted down to her full lips and farther down to her chest. "I didn't come here to mislead you. I have no room in my heart for that kind of love. Not anymore."

"I am over three hundred years old, Damian. I get it." She released her aura, and vivid gold and blue circled her. It caught Lefou's attention as the little Zol Monkey began to reach out and try to grab at the colors. "Get to bed, Lefou. It's time for sleep."

The creature faced her then dropped his head. He hopped off her lap and slowly trotted into the house. She smirked at me, and I rubbed a hand through my hair. "Come, it's late," she said. "I'll show you to your bed."

We walked through the house full of sleeping bodies. She had several bedrooms where the others had gotten comfortable, and she showed me to the living room couch.

"There. I hear it's quite soft," she said as a smile tugged at her lips.

"You're joking. I don't get a bed?"

"Nope. They're all taken."

"What about your bed? It's a king, right? We can both fit there." I gave her my most innocent smile and reached my hand to the side of her waist. I pulled her close to me. She inhaled a shuddering breath as her lips parted in surprise. I didn't give her a chance to respond. I met my lips to hers and felt her soft tongue against mine. She returned my kiss, pressing her hands firmly against my chest and arching her back beneath my fingers that grazed against her. I could tell from the way her golden aura interacted with the blue inner ring that she wouldn't turn me down if I made my move. She had been out here alone for far too long.

I cradled her jaw in my palm, caressing her skin as I held her tightly.

She reached her hand down to mine and grabbed it, pulling me with her to her room. I followed, watching her hips sway inside her loose dress as I thought of nothing else but lifting it off of her.

As we entered her master bedroom, she swept her hands and lit aromatic candles placed around the room. White bedding covered the plush bed, and clothing was mindlessly thrown about the room. But that was of no consequence. Warmth emitted from her as my mouth began to water at the thought of feeling her lips against mine once again. She stood before her bed, staring up at me with molten fire in her eyes.

"Your bed looks incredibly comfortable," I joked, my lips curling into a smile as my blood heated and my dick became taut. I closed the space between us, reaching my mouth to meet hers, and she returned my kiss with her arms reaching around me. I shifted down, planting kisses on her cheek, against the line of her jaw, on the smooth flesh at her neck.

"You know, the stars wrote you here tonight," she whispered.

"Ah yes, Venus is in Taurus this week. Well, I'm more than happy for the timing of our visit," I said as I loosened the string at her back that held the dress up. It fell to the ground, revealing her fully to me. The candles in the room gave away the sensual curves of her breasts, waist and legs, while the shadows made me even more curious. I pulled off my shirt and stood in front of her, the button of my jeans open and my zipper lowered. Her eyes danced around my body, her gaze tracking the lines of my muscles.

Suddenly, she stopped staring and reached for me with frantic need. Her lips fell upon the hard lines of my chest, her hands moving along the contours of my stomach. I fisted her hair and gently tugged her head back, meeting her gaze with mine. Then I lifted her in my arms, wrapping her legs around my waist and tasting her with my lips and tongue. I set her down on the bed and smiled at her predatorily as I hooked my hands around her thighs and spread her legs apart. She gasped with delight as I met my mouth to her inner thighs, gently kissing them until I made my way up to the apex. A desperate moan left her lips as I fell into the wetness that awaited my tongue. I circled her center as the pleasure continued to build. Several more moans left her mouth as I continued to focus on the place that made her arch her back the most. I circled faster, gripping her thighs tightly as I brought her to a climax.

I lifted my head, and my eyes met hers.

"Now. I need you inside me. Right now." Her breath came in rapid pants.

I entered her center, sending a crashing wave of pleasure through me. My muscles tightened and released with every thrust, a light sheen of sweat forming along my skin. I raked my tongue along her neck, then felt her hard nipples in my palm. I moved down, licking her breast as desire and heat coursed through my body. She shut her eyes and released a cry of delight as I continued to rhythmically match the movement of her hips with every thrust. I responded to her cadence, moving as fast as she did, and we crashed over the very edge of our pleasure together.

She laid her head softly on the pillow next to me. Her hands wrapped around my waist as she hummed softly and fell asleep. It was a comfort to be in her arms, knowing the difficult journey that lay ahead the next day. I had heard all the warnings about Xibalba, the place of fright, many times over. But it didn't matter to me at all. Not an ounce of me considered any alternative. I had to at least try, and if the others wanted to follow me to the Underworld, I wouldn't stop them.

— · —

CHAPTER 18

DAMIAN

The sun was just about to set, the light haze covering the yellow sky on the horizon beginning to blend into the blanket of night. We were gathered behind Gaelle's house, in the woods, inside a Zol ring that Gaelle had created by placing rocks in a large circle and painting the twelve zodiac glyphs on them.

"You need to mow your lawn. You can barely see the Zol ring," I grunted.

"The mower's in the shed. You're more than welcome." She held her hand out toward the shed, a teasing glimmer in her eye.

"Sure. I'll get to it when we make the Climb back." I rubbed the back of my neck as I forced myself to remember that this was worth it. I owed it to Sasha to do everything I could to get her out of there. She would do this for me. She would do it for any of us.

"You should know, I've only done one Descent, ever. And I still have no idea how it went for my aunt. If you see her down there, send her my love, will you?"

Jenna's eyes opened wide, and she reached for Lex's hand. He gripped hers tightly.

"That's not true," I said. "What about Mira and Lizbel? They made the Climb that night after you dared them to descend. I was here."

"Oh yeah. That night I was on starfire; I barely remember anything from those days." She laughed nervously, then made sweeping movements with her arms. "Ok. Let's get started."

The bracelets on Gaelle's wrists clicked together as she raised her arms over her head to summon the transcendent energy. A golden glow rose from the stones painted with the zodiac glyphs, and I realized then that she had used mirth color from the Zol Sen. How she had gotten ahold of them, I had no idea. But now I understood how she was able to perform this ceremony. Mirth color was only found in the deep caves of Scorpio Gate, in the most remote desert valley. The colors of the clay rock from that part of the desert were said to also exist inside the caves of Xibalba. The legends said that a colony of giants had mined the colors and brought them to the center of the desert before it was even a desert, and before Xibalba was secluded in the deep folds of the planet. The stories of mirth color were more legend than anything. No one dared to go looking for the mirth color, because it was surrounded by a colony of giant scorpions.

The golden glow hovered behind us as Gaelle's black eyes became wide with wildness. She circled her hands in the air, whisking the glow around us. The charge from the energy felt like static at my back as it connected to my skin. The energy was reaching for me. Gaelle began to chant in the old Celtic tongue, singing her script, which was a spell unique to her and her gifts. It was her ability to live free of the judgment and constraints of this world that made her the perfect channel for this type of spell. The golden glow around us was an extension of her aura, amplified by the mirth color on the rocks. She was enveloping us in her free spirit and light energy so that she could send our Zol anywhere we wanted to go. The glow had grown and began sweeping around us faster and faster. It tugged at my skin with a desire to pull me in. It raised over us and met at the center, forming a moving golden dome over our Zol ring.

"Now close your eyes and release yourselves to the golden Descent," she said, her voice a melody.

I closed my eyes and felt nothing but a slight tug at my back.

"*Leig leam*," she chanted, and instantly we were swept into the golden stream of energy.

It was gold and bright in the big circle that had brought me into its current. Laughter, warmth and joy surrounded me, and I was carried away into memories of my youth. The most fun I'd ever had as a kid, sliding down the waterfalls of House Aquarius where I'd grown up, threatened to distract me. I snapped my fingers as the memories flooded my mind to force myself to focus on the plan. We had to actively think of where we wanted to go in order to travel there.

Gaelle's energy was positive and joyful, and it was the opposite of the Underworld's energy. I had to remember that. I brought forward a memory of Sasha, when I first met her and she had no idea of the fierce creature she truly was. I pictured her held captive by the death gods, and a vision of her began to form in my mind.

She was in the obsidian palace of the god Vucub-Cane. I had found her! I hoped the others had too. As I centered all of my attention on this one thought, I was yanked out of the light and pleasant energy that surrounded me and drawn into a darker place. I began to hear the morbid wails of death in the distance. The stark cries of pain and suffering. This was where I was headed.

Moments later, after traveling in a wind of dark shadow, I landed next to Zayne and Bjorn, who had arrived at the gates of the palace before me. Jenna and Lex arrived just after I did, and I released a ragged breath as I took them in.

"Now that wasn't so bad," I said with a grimace.

"No, it was worse," Jenna replied, tucking loose strands of her curly hair back into her ponytail. Her jade eyes were bright and alert.

"Did you all see Sasha? I'm guessing she's in there, in Vucub-Cane's palace," Zayne said as he looked through the pristine iron bars that formed the entrance gate. Just then, the gate creaked open.

"Should we just walk right in and demand they give us Sasha?" Bjorn asked, his red hair messy from the Descent.

"Yes. Vucub-Cane will already know we're here. There is not a Zol who can enter his Underworld without him knowing about it. We've triggered every ward they have. Rather than sneak around, let's just go to him and demand that he returns Sasha to us. Either that or lose his nagual force." I knew it was risky, but it was the only card we could play.

"Bueno. Vamos," Lex said. *Fine. Let's go.*

And off we went, walking into the deadly unknown.

CHAPTER 19

SASHA

A Zol Troll, who I would learn was one of the many servants at this palace, opened the doors for us. As I entered, the foyer extended up to a three-story ceiling with an obsidian chandelier hanging from its center. Modern décor completed the space. The palace was furnished as a home, with couches, chairs and rugs intricately placed in the large and expansive living rooms at either side of the grand foyer. Yet it wasn't entirely welcoming. The obsidian chimney and stark walls commanded their own sort of spatial power.

Statues of the gods and symbols of the Underworld were displayed in the otherwise normal-looking paintings and art. At the edge of the living room, a soothing waterfall fell over obsidian stones, and narcissus flowers grew around it. Ancient stories were at play with every drop of water that cascaded over those stones and from every item in this home. One just had to look closely to see it.

"What are we doing here?" I asked and went ignored. Until I saw him.

Dark-brown hair fell slightly past thick eyebrows. Full lips rested inside a short brown beard. The contours of hard muscles lay just underneath a fine black shirt. The design of the shirt, and the long length of the hair, were of another time. As I felt his gaze land upon me, my pulse hitched. My dark thirst came alive within me at that exact moment, and I was damn thirsty. I licked my lips. Then he disappeared.

"Who—who was that?" My eyes darted around the room, searching for him. *Did I just imagine that?*

"What did you see?" Vucub-Cane said as he entered the living room. I told him what I'd seen. "Oh yes. He's making himself known to you, now that the time is close."

"Who is making himself known"—then I remembered—"Your Grace?" I searched his face. "And can I get some answers now? Like why you're doing this? Where is my unit? What's happened to them—Your Grace?" My shoulders were raised, and my voice a low growl.

The guards closed the space between us as they pointed their electrical wands at me. I sneered at them as I took a few cautious steps back.

"Like I said earlier, no need for the formalities here. Just relax." Again, his face revealed nothing but slight boredom.

I rolled my eyes and snatched my arm back from the reach of one of the guards.

"If I cared about how you felt, I would feel sad for you. You've won and you don't even know it," Vucub-Cane said.

I scoffed. This situation did not at all seem like I had won at anything.

The death god turned and left the room abruptly, and as he left his vast, cold power followed after him. He gave one final command before exiting, telling the guards to release the restraints around my wrists. The batty-eyed Arcana Angel narrowed his gaze on me and slowly released the cuffs. I rubbed my wrists, red and sore from the charge, and turned my back on the four of them, ignoring them as they left the room.

The troll brought me into a lavish room, equipped with high-end furniture and endless views of an opaque sea with what looked like diamonds at the peaks of each wave. It smelled like the ocean here, although we were in the Underworld deep within the Earth. Fiery-red birds flew over endless dark waves, and all-black shiny seagulls picked at black shells on the sandy shore.

The sound of the door opening brought me back to the present, and I nearly cried when I saw Carly at the doorway. She flashed me her aura, so I knew it was her and not a deception spell. Immediately I gave her a huge hug. She was my shaman's apprentice, and she had helped me in my first ritual when I had become a nagual. Her hair was still as shiny, long and black as I remembered. The shaman's tattoo now decorated her arm in a band of the ancient Zol script, just like Damian's.

"I'm so glad it's you. You've got to help me get out of here. I don't know what the fuck is going on." My eyes searched hers as I approached her. Her body was stiff, her jaw tight.

"You are safe here," she said. "This is exactly where you need be."

I dug my nails into my palms as I realized she was one of them.

"The god, Vucub-Cane, has appointed me as the shaman to preside over the mating ritual. He asked me to visit with you in the days to come for preparations," she said.

"What mating ritual?" I kind of knew what she meant, but this was all so fucked up I needed someone to say outright that I would be mated to the UnZol King so I could protest it, for the record.

"You are mating with the UnZol King, when he returns in two moons," she deadpanned, and I had to consider how I reacted to her. I inhaled a deep, stilling breath.

They're planning another ritual. Yet another transformation.

"Oh yes. Of course." Challenging her was useless at this point. With her I had to use a different approach. "I thought only my shaman could do my rituals."

She smiled coyly, knowing full well why he wasn't here. "We only wish to have supporters at the ritual. Damian has been disconnected from Zol Stria for a long time, not exactly what one would call reliable. I am more than capable of performing the ceremony."

"And you follow the UnZol King?" It was an effort to keep from clenching my fists.

She considered me for a moment. Her black eyes had a smooth shine to them. She was much more confident in who she was and what she was doing than I had remembered her.

"I know what they taught you at the Academy, but it was wrong. The Dark Zodiac may be ruthless, but the Zol Council are murderous hypocrites. They've tried to hide the truth of what they truly are from all of us. But they have failed. We know too much." Her hands were folded in front of her, and her chin was taut.

"What do you mean 'they're hypocrites?'" I released a shaky breath while I scratched at my matted hair and fidgeted with the waist of my white jumper.

"Around two thousand years ago, Zol Stria divided the world into twelve Houses to create a division between each zodiac sign so that if there was war, one couldn't simply walk from one territory to the other. This would have potentially kept damage contained. Allowed reinforcements to isolate battles. But it didn't work. Instead, we had the Faellen Wars, where many innocents were slaughtered. This was because the wars were being fought on the inside of each House. Lords wanted to overtake their Vicars, while the Dark Zodiac used the opportunity to rebel against the way the Zol Council wanted things to be done. They were rebelling against the abuse of power from the lords and governors of the Houses." Her voice remained controlled and unreadable.

"And Dark Vampires were fighting for the right to have humans for dinner," I scoffed. "Everything I've been taught at the Academy, all of our training... The UnZol King created Zolless armies to feast on Fae. How can you be ok with this?" My shoulders tensed. "Plus, I've seen what the Dark Zodiac can do. I know how far they'll go. You know what I went through with Grange. You know what that vampire Solana did to Trent. How can you tell me you want that kind in control?"

She shook her head. "There is still much you don't know about Zol Stria. About the slaves they keep. Slaves like my family. About their righteous control over our lands, the farming of humans... about the way they rule. You have been closed off in the Academy. Not exposed to the realities of this world. You have no idea who or what you serve." Her brows furrowed. "They would have you believe that the Dark Zodiac is to blame for everything that has gone wrong. Yet did you know that in Zol Stria, every firstborn child is taken from the homes of the lesser-born to serve the Zodiac Houses as slaves? That there is only ever any justice for the high-born? This is all the work of the power-hungry politicians of Zol Stria, just like Ixia. All they want is to rule and control, and they will stop at nothing to get what they want," Carly bit out through gritted teeth.

"And you will need to decide very quickly whose side you're on. If there's one thing I know, it's that you should never believe everything you're taught in history books." Her mouth twitched. "It is a fact that the UnZol King has blood on his hands. He was feared and reviled. But he was fighting for us. He will come back and bring true balance by the power of the stars." She released a breath and continued, "Damian found me starving on the streets because I had no parents. He never knew what happened to them because I never told him. But I knew.

"I found out many things when he disappeared from Zol Stria and left me with the Master Zol Shaman who revealed the truth behind the ways of the Vicars and the Council. Through the Wall of Mirrors, he showed me how Zol Stria had taken my parents as slaves all those years ago. The rulers of House Gemini are vampires and feed off the blood of mages like us. They swear it gives them more power. I come from a line of mages and shamans. Zol Stria never cared what happened to me when they left me to die. There are many like the Master Zol Shaman that I studied with. They have been around long enough to know the truth of what the Zol Council is, and what really happened to the UnZol King."

I still wasn't ready to believe her, but I was beginning to see why she believed what she did.

She went on, "What Grange and Solana did back in Colombia was terrible."

"'Terrible?' Grange and Solana are monsters!"

"Grange was a changed human, possessed by a Zol Demon. He was but one of her many soldiers. Those are impossible to control by anyone other than the Dark Zodiac. Solana has grown much more powerful, and she has the relics we need. No matter the monster she may be, we must reach a truce with her," Carly deadpanned. "And she will continue to grow more powerful with or without us. She is the great niece of the UnZol King and the only living heir to his throne. But no matter what she's done over the centuries, she's figured out that she does not have the power to command the legions of UnZol Demons that he does. So, she has stopped fighting for a throne she will never sit on and has decided to instead, form an alliance with Vucub-Cane to bring her great uncle back to us."

Her eyes were resolute as she spoke, yet her words left a bitter taste in my mouth. How could she be so brainwashed? The UnZol King was pure evil.

"And what's in it for the god Vucub-Cane? His brother was the one who locked me up. Does Hun-Cane even know I'm not in Xibalba anymore?" I looked around the room. "Why would Vucub-Cane go against his own brother?"

She sat down at the edge of an armchair and motioned for me to sit across from her. "Sit, please."

I kept my feet firmly planted where I stood. "I'm fine."

She cleared her throat. "Hun-Cane still doesn't know you're gone. As soon as you left, Vucub-Cane placed Eliana as a decoy in the isolation room. She'll be fine. Just a little thirsty for dark energy like you were, but nothing she can't recover from within a few hours after being released."

"You what?" Terror ripped through my chest as I imagined Eliana in that dreary white cell. I approached Carly aggressively, ready for a full-on attack, and she raised a white shield that stopped me in my tracks.

"Now, now, there is no need for aggression."

I shifted my hands to my jaguar claws and took a swipe at the shield, but it did nothing. She'd obviously learned some impressive tricks of her own. I paced the room, considering how hard it would be to run back to the cell and get Eliana out of there. "You didn't answer my question," I told her.

"Vucub-Cane has tried for centuries to convince his brother that he should not support Zol Stria so blindly, with no concessions. He has decided it is time to take matters into his own hands. And with the coming of Pluto, it is time for a new dawn in our world. The Zol Council has refused to accept or acknowledge the Dark Zodiac. Now, they will be forced to see. With the power of the UnZol King, the Dark Zodiac will once again have a voice in Zol Stria. He will unite us all."

I considered her and how she had come to be so sure of herself. So sure of all of this. "Is your mentor, the Master Zol Shaman, part of the Dark Zodiac?"

"No, he's not. Like the god Vucub-Cane, he wants unity in Zol Stria, for all Fae. The Dark Zodiac are not the enemy. What they are is the balance that our world needs. The Light Zodiac cannot exist unchecked and insolation. The dark is just as important as the light."

I grimaced in disbelief. "Do you guys understand the destruction this will unleash on humans if the Dark Zodiac were free to do what they wanted?" I kept my voice calm, though I wanted to yell at her.

"There would be changes in the human world, but certainly not destruction. Think of it more like a restructuring." She was dead serious, and I couldn't believe it. Her shield began to dissipate as we continued our conversation and I had begun to control my emotional reaction to what she was explaining.

"Ok, let's say everything you're saying is true. Why in my right mind would I ever want to mate with the UnZol King? Besides the fact that he's responsible for immeasurable carnage and damage. I don't even know him." I couldn't believe I was even asking that question, but reality had to be faced at some point, very soon.

"Because you are his Zol Mate. When you mate, you mate for eternity. When you see him again, you will know love like nothing else you have ever felt before." Her eyes opened wide in adoration, and a shiver simmered down my spine.

I had only ever heard of Zol Mates in my Celestial Alignment class. My stomach twisted in knots, and it was an effort not to grimace. But there wasn't time to spend agonizing over my recently wrecked love life. I had to focus on finding my way out of this mess.

"And if I refuse to mate with him?" I asked, and it was an effort to keep my voice from choking.

She lifted her chin. "That is not an option."

"It is when I reject the bond," I said firmly.

"You wouldn't want to put your nagual or Damian in danger." Her voice was soft, but her eyes were not.

"You wouldn't." *I dare you.*

She pressed her hand against her chest. "Of course, I wouldn't. But I'm not doing anything." She placed her hand back on her lap. "Vucub-Cane has part of your unit. Bjorn, Jenna, Lex, Zayne and Damian. He thought it would be best if he kept them confined until you were mated. No harm will come to them, rest assured." She pursed her lips, and I wanted to smack her across her pretty face.

My blood began to bubble in desperation. The walls began closing in on me, and the room felt incredibly small. I stood before her and placed one hand on each of the armrests of her chair, caging her in. "How did they find them? And what about the others? Andres and Axel? Where are they?" I asked her, only partially shifting by releasing my jaguar fangs and snarling.

She didn't even flinch, and that was when I was sure she had faced enough monsters of her own that I wasn't scary enough to move her. I raised a stronger deflector and braced myself in case she decided to try and launch me off of her with a magic spell. But none came.

"Yes, they are all fine." Her too-calm tone and demeanor unnerved me as my jaguar claws extended from each finger and dug into the fabric of the armchair. "You should be so lucky to have a unit that will come all the way to Xibalba to save you. And as far as Andres and Axel are concerned, they returned safely to Zol Stria after your failed escape. They have returned to their duties, which were in separate Zodiac Houses. Thanks to Eliana, the Council still thinks you're in Xibalba, right where Hun-Cane put you. All is going according to our plan..." She eyed me expectantly.

I scowled and pushed off the armchair. "All is well, except that Ixia, the Fae who killed my aunt, is back in power, my unit is being held hostage and I'm here against my will." I shifted on my feet as I considered everything that had led to this moment. I thought I would have been more prepared to deal with being cornered like this. After all, I had been through a lot of betrayals already. But then again, nothing could have prepared me for this.

"I thought the UnZol King couldn't come back without all the relics," I said. "Even if you convince Solana to give you hers, Zol Stria isn't just going to hand over the relics they have."

She swept her hands along her lap, straightening her loose black skirt. "Zol Stria doesn't have to hand over anything. Solana is on her way here now, with hers. We have the relics that the Council still believes are in their possession. And here you are, the final piece we need. There's nothing left to do but wait until the time is right." She angled her head forward and gave me a small, satisfied smile, which I didn't return.

This whole time we'd thought the Council had the relics, but instead they were with the Dark Zodiac. More questions rose to the surface, but there were too many chaotic thoughts in my mind to form a coherent sentence. I swallowed air tightly as sweat from worry began to form on my brow.

I barely noticed when Carly stood and went over to the wardrobe on the other side of the room. When she opened the white wooden doors, she revealed several long dresses hanging inside. She pulled out a black dress with the ancient script of the Zol Sen woven in gold along the neck and down the center. The sleeves were long and sheer and so was the material from the bodice to the neck. "This is the gown and the veil you must wear as the Zol Mate," she said.

I folded my arms in front of my chest and raised one eyebrow in protest. Just then there was a knock at the door.

"That must be Senai, the elven seamstress." Carly let in a tall, Oscuri Elf of House Capricorn. Her ears were pointed, and her gossamer clothing—held together at the waist and neck by jeweled onyx clasps—floated from her flesh as though wind billowed around her.

"Senai will fit the dress to your size, and you must wear it every day. The veil is to cover your face until the ceremony. The stars write the path." She hung the dress on a simple hook on the closet door, then approached the hallway to leave before saying, "You're free to roam the house and the garden. There are wards in place, so there is no use trying to run away. Dinner will be served downstairs in an hour." She was about to close the door when she turned her head and said, "You will see what we all see, soon enough."

I barely heard what she was saying as I stared out the window at nothing in particular. This was all starting to sink in, and it was very, very heavy.

— ◆ —

CHAPTER 20

I wore the dress to dinner, only because it was elegant and extremely expensive-looking, and I couldn't help myself. Having your dress customized by an Oscuri Elf was an honor only reserved for the highest Zodiac Council members, the Vicars and Zol Stria singers and actors. After speaking to Carly about it, I learned that the Oscuri Elves were slaves in Zol Stria, but they were once free under the UnZol King.

Wearing the dress itself was transcendent. Power seemed to exude from the material as it slipped over my shoulders and wrapped around me. They could all think that wearing this dress meant I was accepting my fate. However, even if they did think that, they would be wrong. I was only wearing it because I knew it would be an experience like no other, and I didn't want to miss out.

Carly looked at me approvingly as I joined her and the Master Zol Shaman for dinner. I considered not going, but there was too much I needed to learn. Intel wouldn't be gained by sitting alone in my room.

"The dress is exquisite. Is it comfortable?" Carly asked after taking a small sip of her soup.

"Yes, incredibly comfortable. I don't know how they do it." I couldn't help the slightest smile as I thought of the dress. I really did enjoy wearing it. "By the way, where's Vucub-Cane? Isn't he joining us?"

"No, he has no need for food," said the shaman, his steely grey eyes never leaving his bowl of soup.

During the rest of the meal, they explained what was expected of me at the rite, and I nodded my head obediently, knowing full well I wouldn't be obeying shit.

After dinner I was shown to my room. I imagined that the whole of Zol Stria would find out what Vucub-Cane had been planning and come raining down on him any minute, but they didn't. As much as she infuriated me, at least I got some idea of what was going on from Carly, because after speaking to Vucub-Cane all I ever got was riddles. Once in my large, comfortable room I drew a few conclusions of my own.

I figured that Vucub-Cane was still playing both sides. There was no security breach in the prison, because he had replaced me with Eliana, who had a very similar energy to mine. And as far as the other relics, there were any number of ways he could have managed to acquire them over the centuries he had had to plan. Maybe his wards were so powerful they had gone undetected all this time. Especially if they never suspected him. He was, after all, a god and ruler over Xibalba. No one would dare go against him, or Hun-Cane, because they would either risk being sent here for eternity or risk the gods sending one of their worst demons after them.

My blood went cold at the thought of getting mated to a man I didn't even know. A man who was thousands of years old. A man who had brought about the Faellen Wars and was the opposite of all I was taught to defend, protect and fight for as a defender of Zol Stria. Everything about this made my head spin and wrung my stomach in knots.

As much as I tried to get to meditating and searching for the energy from my nagual unit, I came up against that thick black mental wall again. There was so much security in place. All my powers were locked down by that damned death god.

I was restless, and my mind couldn't settle, worried as I was about my unit and getting out of this mess. I decided to take a walk alone in the garden. Light-grey bushes with black flowers lined a paved charcoal walkway. I held the soft leaves in my fingers, marveling at how life could grow all the way down here without the sun. But I knew from my studies at the Academy that there was a system of tiny suns that nurtured the creatures in this vast and complex Underworld.

As I strolled, I passed a very small troll with skin the texture of tree bark and big, round eyes the size of tea saucers. Like me, Zol Trolls had incredible night vision, and they only ever worked in the night. Her agile hands toiled away at short flower beds of red-and-orange flowers that were such a stark contrast to the rich black leaves that held them.

When the troll saw me strolling in her direction, she stopped what she was doing, stood at the walkway and curtsied. "My queen," she said in a raspy voice with what sounded like a thick Mexican accent.

"What? I am not your queen. I'm a nagual, protector of Zol Stria," I answered.

The troll averted her eyes and said nothing else. I didn't want to pry or make her feel bad for being mistaken, so I continued walking. But it bothered me. Everything about this bothered me.

As I turned the corner, around a weeping willow with a cascade of black leaves, I found a small pond with a bench. I sat by the pond to consider my options. My jaguar stirred, and I pulled in dark energy to feed her. It came to me in droves. My frustration gave way to relief when I realized I was not being denied my power here. I fed on all the shadows I could find, trying to pull all remnants of them toward me. Those tiny bits I soaked up were unlike any dark energy I had ever felt before. It was dark energy not generated by fear and frustrations, but from the land itself and the memories of the countless souls that had traveled here.

My jaguar grew strong with all the darkness, and she itched to be unleashed. I unclasped the dress, carefully laying it on a bench, and in three heartbeats my face was covered in fur, my fangs were out and sharp black claws extended from my hands. Six heartbeats later I was on all fours. After years of training at the Academy, my jaguar and I were now one. Unlike when I had first shifted, we were now in perfect sync.

It was time to get the fuck out of here, get Eliana and figure out how to break out the others. Not as a prisoner awaiting a mating sentence, but as a nagual, in control of my own path. Life on my own terms. As I leapt over the garden wall and made my way through the grounds, I headed through tall black-and-grey grassy fields toward the edge of the property. There was only a small stone wall marking the edge. Not at all what I would consider tight security. Either the death god feared no attacks, or there was a powerful ward in place.

"No. No. No. Oh no." I heard a faint voice in the distance. The small dark-haired troll ran toward me with her hand extended. "Not safe. Not safe at all," she said in choppy Spanish, and I turned to look at her. From her height and the way she spoke she reminded me of a toddler. I wondered how old she was.

"Mucho peligro," she said. *Very dangerous.*

I snarled in response, and she took a step back, eyes bulging. She searched the ground for something, then picked up a large rock and threw it over the short stone wall before her. The image I saw of tall, black pine trees split for a moment, revealing an ocean of black-and-orange molten lava. Just before the tear in the illusion closed again, we watched as the stone fell into the lava, disintegrating into ash.

Frustrated, I continued along the edge, searching for a break in the illusion. Any signs of a passage out of here.

"Wait," the troll repeated in a voice I could barely hear. "The only way in or out is through the front entrance," she said in her raspy voice, pointing a stubby finger toward the palace behind me. "The wards can only be lifted by the one who is the death lord Vucub-Cane. Only him."

I turned from her and released a roar before pacing in a circle, my long black tail waving and curling around me. I lurched forward, away from that little troll who was annoying me when she was trying to be helpful. I was pretty tough, but even with the dark shadow energy that made me basically impenetrable, I couldn't survive swimming through hot molten lava. I took off into the distance, my paws pounding against the ground. As much as I wanted out of here, I had to think of my unit. If I did escape, they would pay the price. The thought of them restrained as they were, and me not being able to help them, felt like I was bleeding out from an open wound. I loved my unit like family, and I was happy they had my back. But I never wanted them to be captured like that. Not for me.

But I had to face it, even though it ripped into my soul to admit it. Right now, there was nothing I could do to help them. The moment that death god realized I was gone, my unit would be hurt or even worse, killed. *That's my family he's fucking with.*

But I wasn't going to blame myself for any of this. I hadn't asked to be the Zol Mate of the UnZol King. I hadn't told my unit to follow me across the Gates. They had because I was their family, and that's just what you did for family.

And now here we all were, at the mercy of the death god. When my legs were sore from running and my breath came in rapid pants, I slowed down. I had run in one great big circle and had returned exactly to where I had started. I shifted back into my Zol skin and slipped the dress back on. Dropping my head, I decided to return to my room. One heavy foot was landing in front of another when I sensed that little troll looking at me again, blending perfectly into the night. A large shadow came from behind her as black tree branches reached for her and pulled her close. The troll's mother stared at me with large, saucer-like eyes, and it knew I was the predator it didn't want near her child.

I ignored her and kept moving.

Long black grass swept against my legs and the lights above dimmed to almost nothing, and I contemplated this control that the gods had over us. Their unquestionable power to send us to fight wherever they wanted, however they wanted. The gods' ability to command us at their will and take away all our self-control. In that very moment one thing became abundantly clear: the nagual were not free. This nonnegotiable control over us had to end, and it ended with me. I was not down for eternal slavery as the god's protector.

I would have to find some way out of this, and busting out of here wasn't the solution. It was time to come up with a real plan.

CHAPTER 21

My sleep that night was fraught with nightmares. Visions of my unit held captive, their confusion and worry for me making my blood run thick and my head throb. In fact, I barely slept at all, and woke as soon as light entered the window. It wasn't true sunlight but the light of a million tiny suns that floated just below the high rock that enclosed the Underworld. The tiny suns were much dimmer than the sun of our solar system, held in place between the threads of dark matter that concentrated at the heights of the underground.

Thoughts flooded my mind in the early light of morning, and I took a deep, stilling breath before allowing my worries to get out of control.

Patience. All I would need was a little patience. First thing first: get to know the routine here. The people. Gather intel. Then get the fuck out.

But first, coffee.

After dressing in comfortable jeans, a T-shirt and black high-top Converses, I made my way downstairs to the kitchen and actively had to calm the rage building inside me about being locked up in the dark god's mansion. *Every minute I'm in this place, I'm going to be figuring out how to get out of here.*

Shadows twisted in the corners of the long, wide hallway outside my door, and I pulled them into me. It was interesting how my powers weren't being withheld. I suppose it was because Vucub-Cane, with his omnipotent control over our kind, was around to stop me in my tracks no matter what I tried. And it could be that with the endless ocean of lava they had around the outside of this place, they knew I wouldn't be able to break free. I'd figured out last night that there was an impenetrable ward on the front door, set there by the god himself as though he'd left a part of him in the door to prevent me from leaving. And finally, there was the fact that they were holding my unit hostage until I complied with the mating of the most wicked Fae to have ever existed so I wouldn't be tempted to burn this place down with my fire element.

I passed the demons he kept on as staff, each refined and well-dressed, and entirely unaffected by my presence as one opened the drapes to a two-story window overlooking the black forest outside. Another stacked fresh black wood by the fireplace. I made my way to the breakfast room. I was anxious about this situation, and not hungry at all. But I still decided to eat if only to keep my human side's strength up and sharp as I continued to mull over how I was going to get us all out of this mess. The smell of avocado eggs with toast and applewood bacon made my mouth water. It was my absolute favorite. *How could they possibly know?*

As I entered the kitchen, the demon chef greeted me by way of a nod as he brought my food to the table with gentle care. His limbs were long, his hair thick and pulled back off his face, and he seemed interested in my reaction to his food. Green eyes watched me take my first bite, and when I smiled at him to acknowledge how good it tasted, his thick black wings rustled softly in satisfaction. I finished breakfast and went to lose myself in the massive library I had found while wandering around yesterday.

The library was circular, the books stacked from floor to ceiling on shelves that headed down a spiraling passage to complete darkness down below. I peered over the edge of the rail and couldn't see the bottom. It was as though every book ever written was stored on these shelves. There were sitting areas in carved-out alcoves along the sides, and a few Fae sat there quietly absorbing the content they read. There weren't many. Just a couple Zol Sen that served this House, the omega of the Zol Wolf pack of Xibalba, and then there were the two sphinxes that worked and lived among the books in here. One of the sphinxes approached me as soon as I arrived. When she spoke, her voice was soft and had a slight echo, which rang inside my ears.

"My sorrow moves oceans, tugs at her heart
Though we're bound to each other, we remain worlds apart
Round and round my cell I walk, but never complain
A slave I have been, and shall remain."

I rubbed my chin, remembering the rule about sphinxes—that they only granted entry if you solved their riddles.

The sphinx only waited, expectant.

I had heard this riddle once before. How each of these phrases sounded like me, right now. But I wasn't the answer. It was la luna.

"The moon," I replied.

She moved to the side, allowing me entry into the dark, quiet library.

I was particularly interested in finding books about the Faellen Wars and any information that supported what Carly had told me. When I asked the sphinx where I could find those books, she flapped her massive wings as she lunged her lion feet forward and flew to the section I needed. I headed straight there as she drifted off, somewhere else.

There were all the typical books I had studied at the Academy, and then there was a banned books section. I knew it was banned because it was literally labeled, "Banned Books." I pulled several from the shelves and took them to one of the comfortable alcoves where I began reading. There was so much information I wasn't sure where to begin. I turned page after page, searching for some understanding of who the UnZol King was. Who his mate was back then, or, more like, who I was back then. Just as I shoved away the fourth book with no new information, I reached for the fifth. It was titled *The Unspoken Truth about the UnZol King and the Age of Darkness* and written by the Master Zol Shaman II. The moment my fingers graced the cover and opened it, a cold chill swept across the back of my neck.

All my senses awakened. I pulled my shoulders back, and my eyes began to scan the area for whatever it was that had triggered me. I couldn't sense anything nearby, so I studied the book more closely. From the way the book tingled at my fingertips, I could tell it had a signaling ward on it. This was a ward designed to alert someone as soon as the cover opened.

One of the two sphinxes flew down from the top floor and registered me holding the book. I shrugged my shoulders and smirked at her. She nodded, lifting the ward with a wave of her paw, and then fluttered off. My curiosity was piqued.

What is in this book?

Before I could even begin reading, the shadows began closing in on me faster than I could absorb them. Absorbing shadows had become an unconscious process at this point. Most of the time I just absorbed as I went about my day, instinctively drawing on the dark energy around me just as humans absorbed sunlight and turned it into vitamin D. I never felt "full" or tired of absorbing the darkness. I simply drank it in unconditionally and used it as I channeled my elemental magic or shifted into my jaguar form.

But this dark energy was so overwhelming and all-encompassing that I had to lift a deflector spell to slow it down. It was as though I was pulling in the shadows to shift into my jaguar form, only I wasn't trying to shift. I was just sitting here, reading.

What the fuck is happening right now?

I stood up, bringing the book along with me as I searched for somewhere to go to get away from whatever this was. I found a long hallway off to the side of the main walkway and tried a few of the doors. I was several feet ahead of the cloud of mist as it tumbled over itself on its way toward me. I just needed a second to think. Finally, one of the ornate wooden doors opened, and I immediately shut the door behind me and looked around. The room smelled of sandalwood and incense, and there were statues and pottery in clear encasements.

A smaller sphinx flew toward me, and she landed on the ground. She seemed ancient; wrinkles lined her face, and the skin on her lion paws sagged. Sphinxes lived for centuries, and she must be at least three hundred years old. "My queen." She bowed. "He awaits you in the main chamber."

"First of all, I'm not your queen. And exactly who is waiting for me?"

"Our king."

I shook my head. "Your king. Not mine."

The shadows seeped in from the top and bottom corners of the door, closing in around me again. I stepped backward, walking away from them. Their shape and form seemed threatening. Intense. I didn't want to be surrounded by something I didn't understand. If my supposed mate had sent this dark mist to corner me into his room, I would go in there and let him know what I really thought about all this. And I was sure he wouldn't like it.

I wasn't up for whatever stupid game he was playing. I stomped toward where she said the chamber was, and I soon realized I was entering the room from a back entrance. This was a grand chamber room of another part of the house. Columns led up at least two stories high, so the room was spacious and open. Black-and-red plants were carefully placed in tall floor vases around two black couches and chairs. Sand-colored floors and walls brought a touch of warmth to the straight lines of the walls and furniture. I gazed around the space, not knowing what to expect until everything felt still.

Then I saw him, and the air was sucked out of the room. I couldn't hear a sound, I couldn't feel a sensation except for the lack of it. I was in a vacuum, and my gaze was locked on him.

I knew those eyes. I knew those shoulders. I knew the scar on the right side of his face. A scene replayed in my mind: a knife dipped in ash flew at his head as he ducked just in time to miss the full blow. Then I was overwhelmed with a feeling of gratitude because afterwards he was in my arms, and rather than dying from the knife thrown at him, he had only received a cut that bled for days.

Scene after scene played over in my mind as hidden memories with him came forward. We fought in the Faellen Wars, side by side until we were both covered in blood and sweat. Somehow, I knew that he could shift into three different forms. That he wielded three elemental powers: water, earth and air. That he was the most powerful Fae to have ever been born. And when we mated, I brought the fourth element of fire so that together we would be a force of all four elements. We were both created by the Zol Gods, and created for each other. And then I was reminded of an agonizing hurt that crushed my very soul when I learned he had been captured and killed. The excruciating pain in my heart lasting for the decades of my life after.

I was flooded with emotions of love, angst, frustration, passion and pain. It was almost too much to bear as a silent tear slipped down my cheek. My legs almost betrayed me in their urge to run toward him and wrap my arms around him, to finally feel him against me again after centuries of separation. But my will was stronger, and I remembered exactly who I was. I held myself back.

This could all be a spell. A wicked trick of deception just to get me to fall into whatever scheme this was to bring down terror in this world. A spell of magic I couldn't detect, because all I sensed and all I felt was the familiar dark energy that fed me my power and strength and fueled my elemental magic. I was in unfamiliar territory, and I was beginning to get the feeling it was all way over my head.

CHAPTER 22

He just stood there, his essence something between spirit and flesh. Somehow in this realm of physical matter, and yet still in another. His eyes locked on me as though he knew me. And it was very strange, because at once I was drawn to him, and yet in this life, as Sasha Moreno, I didn't know him at all.

"What do you want from me? Why are you here?" My voice was ragged, and my tongue felt heavy, cumbersome as the words fumbled out of my throat.

He simply stared at me, a ghost that could not speak. *Still not of this world. Can he not form sounds?* He was wearing that same fine black shirt I had seen him in the first time. His golden skin gleamed in the light of day. His lips parted as though he wanted to speak, but no words would come.

"I refuse to mate with you. I don't know what all this is about, but I am not into it. In fact, I just want to leave here and free my unit. That's all I want." I crossed my arms in front of my chest, knowing that there was so much more I wanted. So much more I needed to know about what I was feeling for him. But I kept all of those thoughts to myself. This whole thing was confusing enough as it was. "So, at the rite, when they ask me to become the Zol Mate of the deadly UnZol King, I think you should know I'm going to say 'no,' so don't get your hopes up."

He tilted his head as a playful look flitted across his face as his eyebrows creased.

I know that look! It drove me crazy, but that look meant he wasn't taking me seriously. Not only did that look infuriate me, but it made me want to cover him with kisses at the same time. I scoffed and turned away from him. I had to remember who he was. The evil, Dark-Zodiac-supporting monster that had spawned the destruction of Zol Stria and propelled nothing but pure-evil, flesh-eating creatures into the human world. Memories of his brutality were also returning, and I remembered that he was the mastermind behind the uprising of Fae against Fae. Then, my mouth curled into a smile as an ancient, forgotten, intimate memory of us washed over me, and I decided to try something.

I faced him again and began taking slow, measured steps forward. As I got closer, I searched his deep black eyes, his full lips, his perfect face. The closer I got, the more the dark mist around him lifted, and, somehow, he seemed more human and less like an apparition. He stood a whole foot taller than me, and I had to raise my face up to look at him. I had never seen a man more beautiful, his features perfectly etched out of a dream. I reached my hand to touch his arm, to see if there was anything solid under the shadows that were forming him, and my hand went right through. There was nothing at all. He wasn't physical matter, and, despite the resistance from my mind, my heart ached at not being able to feel him.

I blinked a few times as I realized how close I was to him. I needed to learn what he was, to find his vulnerabilities. To see if there was any way to convince him that this was all a bad idea. But all that stood in front of me was the phantom of a man that I somehow both knew and didn't know. He tried to caress my cheek with the back of his hand, but all I felt was the lightest brush of air against my skin.

I took two long steps back. "So, you're coming back to life in just two moons, and I'm just supposed to marry you? Don't you realize how ridiculous this is?"

He shook his head no.

"Of course you wouldn't think this is ridiculous, but I do. You should know, I'm in love with someone else. Deeply, madly in love." I was still in love with Trent. Even though I knew we had grown apart over the past few years. Even though he had betrayed me by sleeping with Solana while we were still together. And even though I didn't want to speak to him ever again. I still loved him. It was true.

His shadows seemed to darken; he turned and looked away as though this information hurt him.

I didn't care. I didn't even know him.

Slowly, the room began to fill with the rolling shadows once again, and, as easily as breathing, I called tendrils of the mist toward me. Even more memories flooded into my mind. Memories of a time before I knew of Zol Stria, before I had shifted into my jaguar form. When I was lost and afraid for my life. A time when the shadows showed me my future. This felt the same. As though these shadows were speaking to me directly, showing me things I could not otherwise see.

I looked over at him, and he simply stared at me, unable to speak. But I knew what to do; it was the only thing I could ever do when my emotions overpowered me and my thoughts began to confuse me. I would listen.

I sat on the black leather couch in the center of the room. Instead of calling the shadows into me, or blocking them away, I simply sat and allowed. I didn't try to do anything. I opened myself up to listen. If he wanted to kill me, he would have already. Maybe I could communicate with him somehow, with my mind, through this black mist that surrounded us. It was worth a try and my only hope to convince him to let me go.

I closed my eyes and slowed my breathing, simply allowing the thoughts to pass through me.

The mist was gentle as it surrounded me. I had more than enough stores of dark power, so I stopped pulling it in. When I stopped absorbing it, I began to have a vision:

He was with a woman, each wrapped in one another's arms. He kissed her, and she returned the kiss. She looked much like I looked right now, in fact I could only note the difference from her clothing. When I looked at her, it felt like I was looking at my own long black hair, my deep olive skin, my determined green eyes. However, I could tell that the woman, who looked just like me all those thousands of years ago, was in love with the man in this vision, the UnZol King. She grasped him by the collar and pulled him in closer. Her body reacted to the touch of his hand as he caressed her back. They were in the bedroom chamber fitting of a dark lord, entwined in a passionate embrace that would soon lead to much more than kisses and caresses.

But just as he laid her down on the bed and caged her in his arms, there was a loud crash at the door as it flung open.

They both turned to look at who entered. It was one of his generals. "Zol Stria's forces are approaching. We must prepare for battle. Now, my lord."

Both of them got up, calling every sliver of the darkness surrounding them as though inhaling full, deep breaths of power through every pore of their bodies. It was instant, automatic, and they did it while yanking on leather pants and strapping on knifed belts. Their clothes were of another time: dark, elegant, ornate battle gear. They fell into step together as they left the room, moving at a fast pace down the hallway to the war room. A large map formed the center table, and the general began moving pieces into place to show where the army was coming from.

"Somehow, they channeled the trine of Pluto and Mars to create a crease in the outer ward," the general said. "Celestial Zol Wolves made it through, and they attacked our villages. By the time the trine is over the crease will be wide open and the rest of the army will get through."

The UnZol King looked to the ancient version of me, who had a determined look on her face.

"We have to get everyone inside the castle walls. Is the army ready?" I asked the general.

"Yes, they're taking their positions now. But we don't have enough warriors. Their army outnumbers ours," General Anton said.

With the next deep inhale of dark shadow memories, I remembered who he was. Anton was a true alpha who refused to kill his father to become the leader of the pack, so his father had had him banished. The UnZol King took him in, like all the other outcasts of Zol Stria, and after fighting side by side for centuries, the UnZol King had given him a place to lead, a place to belong, and a place to form his own pack of soldiers.

"Then we will create an army. We will raise the dead," said the UnZol King as his eyes darkened.

"Are you sure that's the only way?" I shook my head. "We can't control them."

"They will kill all of us, negra. What about the children you saved? Those half-human Fae they wanted to destroy? Then there's the barren women. Will you have their mates kill them to free them of their burden as they have for decades? And those mages that've mastered the ridiculously forbidden dark magic? The animals that were trapped for eternity in the depths of the Underworld simply for helping the Dark Fae escape slavery, torture and death? They want to oppress the dark. To control us. Now, will we let them have their victory or will we use our strength to fight them and survive?"

I felt my fire rise as he spoke, knowing there was truth in the words he told this ancient me. That those were my beliefs too, and that believing otherwise could be the greatest lie of my life. The truth that lingered beneath the surface of my soul was right here. This is what the UnZol King was really fighting for, and I began to wonder if all this time, I had been wrong.

The vision faded. Thoughts, memories and sensations from inside the dark mist ceased, and all I was left looking at was the back of my black eyelids. I slowly opened my eyes and looked around the room. He was gone, and I was alone.

CHAPTER 23

On the round, clay coffee table in front of me was the book I had picked up earlier. It seemed to call to me, and I reached for it, feeling a slight stinging static charge as soon as I did. I flipped through the pages, where zodiac symbols, images and text shared the untold stories of Zol Stria. I turned to the pages of the Faellen Wars, which were told from a different perspective, coinciding with what Carly had told me. These books explained that the UnZol King had created the legions of Zolless armies to fight in the Faellen Wars, but only because he needed an army to protect the outcast, banished and rejected Fae of Zol Stria.

Soon after he created enough Zolless for his army, a new comet passed over the planet, one that had never passed through before and has never returned. With the passage of the comet, the Zolless became unruly. He led those he could, but it became impossible to control them all.

He had to adapt. To learn even more about the magic of dark energy in order to channel its power so he could command the Zolless and lead them away from the villages and the families they began to pillage. As he did, he worked closely with the god Vucub-Cane, and together they created the nagual, creatures that could channel the dark energy and protect humans and Fae alike from those who wished to harm them.

The UnZol King turned his focus to controlling the Zolless, and he was captured before he could overtake Zol Stria's Council. For centuries his followers searched for a leader who could give them a new rebellion, where the lesser Fae would no longer be slaves and rejected shifters could still have their place. The Fae now believed that the only way they could achieve their freedom was through the return of the UnZol King.

I closed the book. The story disturbed me. Knowing more of his motivation, more of the circumstances behind everything that brought me to this moment, made me doubt what I thought I knew. I didn't hate him as much as I did before. In fact, an unknown, unfamiliar part of myself felt the very opposite of hate. I was deep in thought about the mysterious UnZol King when Carly entered the room. *Does he even have a name?*

"Well, there you are. I've been looking for you."

My eyes opened wide in surprise at her sudden appearance.

"Solana just arrived with Trent. They are calling a meeting in Vucub-Cane's conference room. Please join us there. You must wear your gown."

I looked down at my T-shirt and jeans. Carly's eyes narrowed, and her teeth clenched. She could scowl all she wanted; she was just going to have to get over it. "Nope, I'm fine like this. What's this meeting about?"

My heart thudded in my chest knowing Trent was here and with *her*. Was he just going to flaunt his romance with Solana in front of me, like it was no big deal? I mean, this was some seriously twisted shit. I had killed Grange, her second-in-command, and right afterwards she had turned Trent into a Dark Vampire, and now he was her number two. *How are we supposed to have a civilized meeting when she's the focus of all my rage and I just want to rip her to shreds?*

I would have to keep my emotions in check big time in order to face them both right now.

I entered the conference room, which was on the third floor of this massive house-palace. Large windows allowed views of the fake forest of black pines, the snowcapped black mountains in the distance and a creamy crimson-and-orange sky. The views were spectacular, if only an illusion that covered the black tar lagoon behind it. Two white couches with an elegant black coffee table and a long, black marble conference table with twelve chairs completed the room. The table had the zodiac wheel in the center, and that table alone looked like it weighed several tons.

There on the right sat Solana, who was next to Trent, and the death god Vucub-Cane sat at the head of the table. As soon as Carly entered, she sat to the left of the death god. And seated at the couch in silent prayer was a Zol Sen, only this one wore a black robe instead of the traditional white robes I always saw them in. From what I could see of her face she was young, her skin glowing and soft, her lips red and ripe, and her eyes bore the golden marks of the ancient Dark Zodiac. *She better keep praying if she thinks Solana is coming out of this room alive.*

I turned my attention to Solana. Her red hair fell in thick waves around her shoulders, and while her face revealed an age no more than twenty-seven, her eyes told of centuries of deceit and suffering. I couldn't even believe I had to be in the same room with her. Then my eyes darted to Trent, whose face was void of emotion, as though he felt nothing at all.

"Sasha, please sit." Vucub-Cane motioned to the chair in front of me, at the other end of the large conference table. His dark tendrils of shadow swirled around me, indicating where to go, and yet my feet remained planted in their place. "We've invited you here to this meeting because Solana would like to call a truce. Join us."

As the death god spoke, I felt my skin prickle. Knowing the amount of control my oppressor had over me, I yanked the chair out from under the table and threw myself into it defiantly.

"The time is nearing for the rite, and as the day of our fateful event grows closer, we have invited the heads of the Dark Zodiac here to coordinate our efforts to unite all of Zol Stria. But before we do, we need to be sure you will be cooperative."

Somehow the voice of this god rang through to my center, and I was overwhelmed with the need to listen to him. It was the way they controlled us. It was his power as a death god. He waved his hand, and one of his Zol Demons, wearing a perfectly tailored Armani suit, moved to the wall and pressed a button. A large projector dropped from the ceiling to reveal my unit. Damian, Zayne, Bjorn, Jenna and Lex were each wearing the white jumpers of Xibalba and being held in a group holding cell in the prison. I knew they could hold their own down there, but they weren't free.

"You have no right to hold them. They didn't do anything wrong. Let them go." My voice was calm, controlled. I knew better than to start off by yelling at the death god who had created me. It would get me nowhere. Better to show him I would be cooperative.

"Solana has had"—he turned to her for a heartbeat, then looked to me again—"a lot on her hands. You must understand, she is a powerful ally of the Dark Zodiac and has raised the largest army in support of our efforts to bring the new era of Stars and Shadows. With the mating rite just two moons away, we need to rein in emotions and move conflicts to the side, for the greater good." The god was not asking; his words were commanding.

My eyes flickered over to Trent, who sat back in his chair and rubbed the back of his neck. His expression gave nothing away, and it made my heart feel like it was tearing into pieces. How could we have even come to this? The table began to warp in my mind, stretching and getting longer, and the three empty chairs between us now felt like thirty.

I turned my head to look at the death god. "Why would I do anything for the Dark Zodiac? They've done absolutely nothing for me."

"In that, you are wrong."

I knew the death god was speaking to me, but I ignored him. I glared at Trent instead. "Trent, is this really what you want? You want us to be over? Are you in love with her?"

He stiffened, then answered, "I want what is best for all of us, Sasha. And we can't go on like this. Solana and I..." He looked to her, and I caught a glimmer of genuine affection in his eyes. It ripped right into my soul. "Together we are a far lesser evil than what would be otherwise. I promise you, I never wanted to hurt you. I just want what's best. For all of us."

And just like that, in less than a blink, I climbed upon the table and launched myself at the infamous leader of the Dark Zodiac, Solana DeSalles. Still in my human form, I allowed my sharp fangs to extend from my mouth and my black jaguar claws to jut out of my fingers, cracking the oak table underneath me. I snarled at her, and she stared at me, her expression giving away some shock at my action, but no fear.

"I am not your enemy," she said. Her tone was all business. "We've had our differences, yes. But he chose me after all, and you're just going to have to deal with that rejection. I could have had your unit killed many times over. But time and again, I have allowed you and your unit to live. So, in fact, ever since Miami I have not wanted to be your enemy. Instead, I want you to be my queen when you mate with the UnZol King. So, let's be friends, shall we?"

I searched her eyes for lies, deception, the faintest glimmer of deceit. In this half-shifted form, I could tap into my jaguar's senses to smell her fear.

I sensed no lies now. I growled at her, then jumped off the table. By some small miracle I was able to control my rage. I stormed off, out of the room.

The death god yelled at me as I walked away, his voice like thunder, "We are not finished."

"Oh yes, we are." I slammed the door behind me.

CHAPTER 24

I took twelve steps down the hallway when I stopped in my tracks.

No, this is not the end of our conversation, I thought to myself.

I turned around and stomped back into the room. Sure, I felt like a sixteen-year-old getting her heart broken all over again. In this case, the hot, handsome, alpha-hole boyfriend had chosen the sexy vampire leader instead of me. All my past insecurities, desperation and fears had risen to the surface in an explosive mess. But I was older now and had been through a lot of shit. Some may consider me much wiser. I had to get a grip and handle this better than my much younger self would.

I swung the door open and approached the large table once again. "If I accept this truce, and put this whole thing behind me, will you release my unit? I want them to be set free, right now. And I want to see them. In person." I wasn't going to budge on this.

The death god looked to Solana and Trent. Their stone-cold expressions revealed nothing. It must be some sort of vampire skill to be utterly emotionless at any given moment.

"We still need to be sure you will mate the UnZol King at the rite," he said.

"Fine. I will mate the UnZol King at the rite. Just let them go. Right now." If I couldn't be free to do what I wanted, at least they should be. It wasn't right for them to have lost all their freedom just because of me. And just maybe I wouldn't have to keep the promise of the mating entirely.

"You are not being truthful," the death god growled. His grey eyes narrowed on me as his fingers slid into his palm where it was resting on the table. It was such a subtle movement, but for all his self-control and composure, it was enough to show he was gravely displeased with my plan to deceive him. He and his brother demanded that the nagual were loyal servants to their gods, and my behavior was nothing close to acceptable for my station. He waved his hand, and two of his mafia-looking Arcana Angels stepped out from the corners.

"They will be taking you back to your room, where you will remain until you come to terms with your fate," he announced.

I shifted on my feet as my mind raced. I really just wanted my friends to be free.

Before his two angel thugs could lay a hand on me, I stomped ahead of them and made it back into my room without them having to touch me. Shortly afterwards, when I was pacing in my room, I heard a knock at the door. I swung it open to reveal Trent standing there, his sad blue eyes fixed on me. My heart couldn't sink any lower than it had, so I just stood there, staring at him.

"What do you want?" The words came out in a shaky breath as I tried deeply to keep my emotions from spinning out of control.

"To apologize. I never meant to hurt you." His voice was deep and sincere. He was hurting, too. I could tell.

"All I want to know is why you kept this from me. If you weren't in love with me anymore, why wouldn't you just tell me?" I bit out at him. Anger was the only emotion I could allow right now. Fuck feeling sad.

"Because I didn't know how to tell you. I never fell out of love with you, Sasha. I just... changed. I'm not the same person I used to be. I don't feel things like you do. My heart is colder now. It's hard." He shook his head, as if at a loss for words.

I stomped back inside my room, and he entered, closing the door behind him.

"And how can you even be with her, after what she did to our unit?" I demanded. "She killed them!"

"She did. And I can't forgive her for that in principle. I know it was wrong what she did. But also, I don't feel anything about that. I'm not angry. I'm not sad. And this is to say, I will never, ever feel as happy as I did when I was with you. It's impossible. My heart, I don't even know if it's in there anymore. But I can remember what it felt like to be happy. To be loved. That's why I kept trying to make us work. I wanted to feel like I did in my memories. But I haven't. Not for a long time." His blue eyes searched mine. "From what I know about mates, you have a chance to find that kind of happiness again. I want you to have that. It hurst me to say this but that's something I can't give you and I'm so sorry."

He infuriated me with every word.

"How can you give up on yourself like this? I've heard of vampires loving again. Feeling happy. That's a load of bullshit, and I can't believe you're buying it." I crossed my arms in front of me.

"I've tried. I went to a seminar on it, at House Aquarius. They gave us all these meditations and mantras. I worked with a therapist and still, nothing happened. I have nothing left. They say that this can happen to vampires if you're turned while you carry a lot of sadness. After my mom died, I just never felt right again, and the sadness turned to numbness. I'm numb to just about everything that happens around me, except I can remember the feelings I had for you." His eyes caught the light as he studied my face. I had read about vampires that felt the same way he was describing. As much as it hurt, I would have to begin to wrap my head around the fact that it was over between us.

"I want you to be happy, Sasha. I think you can be I think you can help make a lot of people happy. If you just see what we're trying to do by bringing back the UnZol King. I don't know what kind of lies they've been feeding you at the Academy, but it's very different from what we learn on the street. He's the only one powerful enough to fight for us, and he's the only one people will follow. We need him."

I flung myself down in the armchair. With my elbows on my knees, I placed my head in my hands. "My whole life, I had no idea about this whole other world called Zol Stria. Now I have to decide if I'm going to be mated to a man from a past life and to fight for a people that I didn't even know were suffering. It's just a lot to ask, and I don't know what to make of it all. To top it all off, the only man I've ever truly loved is breaking up with me." Salty tears began to swell in my eyes, and I slapped them away before giving them a chance to spill down my hot cheeks.

Trent came over and draped one arm around me. I leaned into him and let the tears flow softly into the fabric of his shirt. "I only wish I could even feel sad again," he said. "As you do now. Even your sadness is a gift. It's better than feeling nothing. Figure out what you feel. What it is your heart tells you, about all of this. It knows the way," he reassured me. He held me for a while longer, until my breaths came in a steady rhythm, and I began to understand that I had lost him.

"You better go," I said after I lifted my head from his firm chest and stood up. My eyes and cheeks must have been red and blotchy after all those tears. He stepped in closer to me and placed a cool kiss on my forehead.

"But just think, Trent. She did this to you. She gave you an eternity of not feeling anything at all. How can you turn around and be with her after all she's done to you?" It sounded awful and it explained a lot, why he was capable of having cheated on me, especially with that terrible woman.

"Because with her, I do feel something. The bond we have, she as my maker, allows me to feel her emotions. It's all I have left."

"That sounds like a horrible existence to me," I muttered under my breath.

My thoughts lingered on him for some time after he left the room as my heart lay ripped in shreds at the bottom of my chest. I took in a deep inhale, then another until I got up and made my way back down the hall. I swung open the double doors to the conference room to find the three of them sitting with wineglasses at the couch in the lounge area.

"Fine. Fine..." I raised my hands so my palms faced the god Vucub-Cane. This wasn't about me anymore. It was about my unit now. I had to put the others before myself. "Let my friends go and I will *willingly* mate with the UnZol King."

I knew this was the right decision, because after all, the stars wrote my path and no matter how much I had tried to get out of this shit show, I kept being sucked in deeper and deeper. At this point, it didn't seem I had much of a choice, so I might as well get my friends' freedom out of it.

CHAPTER 25

I guess they were giving me time to heal my shattered heart, because no one came to visit me for some time. The next day I slept later and slumped around my room until I decided to try on the dress again, just for the hell of it. I put it on and twirled around in it. I could be anything in this dress. I could be the most powerful woman in the entire universe. At least I felt like I could. The black opals sewn into the seams and edges were placed there by no human or machine. Only the Oscuri Elves could create such delicate detail from the shadows. They say that the very essence of the dark mist that feeds Dark Fae like me is made into the matter that forms the fabric of the dress. The buttons that held the dress together were none other than the black diamonds from the inside of the live volcanoes of House Leo, delivered to the Oscuri Elves by the phoenix. They were the only Fae who could fly over the heat. This was so much more than a dress. It was moving art.

I sighed and was about to take it off when I changed my mind. Instead, I would wear this to visit Vucub-Cane and ask him where my friends were. It had been two days and I still hadn't seen them. If he went back on his word, I would refuse to go to the rite, and I knew he didn't want that. *He better not fuck with me.*

I pulled my thick black hair into a round bun at the top of my head and carefully brushed in place any loose hairs. Like my villa at the Aries Academy, this room had a bathroom stocked full of every kind of makeup and accessory a girl could dream of, and I went to work making up my face. When I was ready to leave, I pulled the black veil down over my eyes and sought an audience with Vucub-Cane. After searching for him at his office and conference room, I made my way down to the anteroom. The energy had become thick with excitement. Familiar voices filled the space, and the emptiness in my heart began to fill once more.

"Jenna. Jenna!" I exclaimed as I ran toward her.

She turned her deep green eyes to me, but hesitated.

As I reached my hands up to the veil to pull it back over my head, Carly stepped forward from the back of the room, two Arcana Angels flanking her. "Ahem. You are not to reveal your face until the ceremony."

"What's the point in that? They already know what I look like," I snapped at her.

"The stars write the path," she simply said.

"I agreed to be his mate. I didn't agree to being a viuda, and I've got to tell you that this veil does in fact make me look like a widow." I lifted it up, and as soon as Jenna's eyes met mine, she opened her arms for a warm embrace. I squeezed my eyes shut as I hugged her, and when I slowly opened them again, I demanded hugs from Bjorn, Lex and Damian, relieved they were all here, unharmed.

"We've been so worried," Jenna said. "We had no idea what had happened to you. What do you mean you agreed to be his mate, and why are you wearing that?"

Jenna might have asked the questions, but it was clear they were one everyone's mind as my unit looked at me for a response.

"I'll leave you to your conversation," Carly said as she slipped out the back of the room.

Unfortunately, the Arcana Angels remained, hovering as if there was even anything they could do to restrain me and my unit if we decided to turn on them. I felt even more powerful around my pack, knowing that together we could take down anyone we wanted. Even those two uptight dickwads.

"So, when do we eat?" Bjorn grunted after flopping all two hundred and forty pounds of himself down on the couch and kicking his feet up on the coffee table.

"They didn't feed you well at the prison?" Sarcasm laced my tone. "I'll have Amir prepare something for us right away." I gave instructions to the kitchen and returned to the anteroom, eager to catch up with everyone. As soon as I got back, I filled them in on the switch with Eliana, my agreement to do the rite, what I had learned about the UnZol King, and what had happened with Trent and Solana.

"They have Eliana," Zayne grunted, and I nodded somberly, my eyes darting to the guards at the door. His first thought would be the same as mine, which was getting her out of there. But the only way to get her out of there would be through a negotiation, not an escape.

Jenna's eyes narrowed, then she turned to me. "Girl, how are you holding up? That's a lot to deal with." Jenna rubbed my arm, and I just wanted to lay down in my bed, hug her and cry on her shoulder like I used to do during our days off at the Academy. These people were my family. We all had cried plenty of tears for the heartache of leaving the ones we loved on the other side of the Gates.

I looked over at the Arcana Angels, who had Fae hearing. I lowered my voice and raised a tight deflector spell. "It hurt, but I knew it was bound to happen. Ever since Trent became a vampire, he's changed so much, and the truth is, so have I. We grew apart, and it hurts to say it, but we weren't going to make it anyway. What hurts the most is that he decided to stay with that immortal ice bitch."

"Yes, food!" Bjorn said as Amir and his servers entered with several trays of sandwiches, fruit and finger foods.

I got up and poured a whisky on ice from the small bar at the side of the room. "Here, Damian, for you." I handed him the glass, and he swished around the liquid, took a sniff, and whispered a quick spell to release any enchantments.

"I was worried about you," he said, his tone and eyes serious and concerned.

"Oh yeah? Well, I was worried about you," I said, nudging him with my shoulder. We had certainly come a long way from the days when he didn't worry about me at all. But I no longer thought of those days. It was good to have him in my life now, exactly as he was.

As we casually ate, drank and spoke to one another, we sent each other hidden signals through the slightest of gestures. It began with the hugs. Just by the way I passed my hand along their shoulders and the amount of time we squeezed each other, I was sending them messages and they were replying. We were Zol Stria's elite fighting force, and we had come up with our own covert language for situations such as this one. We knew that under the watchful eyes of the Arcana Angels, who read lips and were rumored to be the only creatures capable of penetrating deflection spells, among their many talents, we wouldn't be able to speak freely. And even if they weren't in the room, none of us trusted the gods who had created us, especially after they'd both used their unchecked power to control us.

Through our hidden dialogue, I could also tell that we all felt the same way about our lack of free will as nagual of the twin gods. None of us were happy with the power they both had over us since all of this had started. We agreed, through the passing of a hand over a specific finger, and the raising of an eyebrow after a carefree nudge, that we would form a plan of escape, and it would happen tonight.

I didn't care what I had promised the god Vucub-Came. I didn't care if he would come after me and drag me back to this place. He and his entourage of Arcana Angels, Oscuri Elves, Zol Trolls and Demons needed to learn that we were not theirs to command.

CHAPTER 26

The god Vucub-Cane would be out for the coming days. He was off to work with his brother on the Rot in Gemini Gate. When I pressed Carly about how they'd managed to keep Hun-Cane from suspecting what was going on here at the palace, she explained that Vucub-Cane had created the Rot that was spilling over between Gates to distract his brother and keep him out of Xibalba until the UnZol King's return. However, it had begun to consume entire territories, and all the Council members were trying to find ways to contain it. I thanked Zol for giving them a distraction and getting the god Vucub-Cane out of here when we needed it.

"There will be double the Arcana Angels in the palace and outside now that the god Vucub-Cane isn't here," I whispered to Damian.

He only blinked once and smirked, being sure not to give anything away to the guards in the anteroom.

Just then, Carly entered. Her lips pursed as though she had just tasted a lemon. "Hello, Damian." Her words were short. Pointed.

"Carly, what a surprise." He flashed his most captivating smile and approached her. He greeted her in the Mexican tradition with a quick peck on the cheek. "They didn't tell me you'd be here." His warm reception of her would have surprised me, but I knew him too well for it to be believable. He was being charming to win her over and gain her trust. I bet he was just hoping that if he did, she would let her guard down.

But even though I knew his motives, I could help but be annoyed by it. I pulled the veil over my face in an effort to hide a very obvious eye roll that would have been impossible to prevent. It's not that I didn't like Carly. In fact, she could be right about what she was telling me about the UnZol King, and, if anything, I admired her ambition. But as far as I was concerned, she was standing between me and my freedom. I was being forced to do something without any concern for what I wanted, and if she were a good friend, she would be helping me escape so I could make my own decisions about what was right in this situation.

She was happy to keep me trapped here, forced into this mating that I didn't want and didn't ask for. And she hadn't made any effort to help me get Damian and the rest of the unit out of prison. That made her one of them. But between now and the moment we all busted out of here, she had to believe we were all on the same side.

"I'm happy to see you made the Descent all in one piece," she replied shortly.

"So am I," he chuckled. "I hear you will be facilitating the rite. Congratulations. There aren't many mating rituals held these days. Not since the Faellen Wars. I'm looking forward to seeing you in action." He swished his whisky, and she stole a glance at it, perhaps remembering that we were once all on the same side and that she was the one who had gotten lost along the way.

"Thank you. Well, you all must be exhausted," she said, gesturing to my unit. The others had entered into casual conversations between themselves, careful not to reveal any alarm or dissatisfaction with the current situation.

"Yes, I'll show them to their rooms. Thank you, Carly." My tone was dismissive, which was pretty much the way I'd been treating her since I'd arrived in the death god's palace.

The first room was Damian's.

"The palace is beautiful," he said.

"Yes, it is a wonder." I lowered my voice and leaned in. "There's an illusion spell around the perimeter. It's surrounded by a lava field. The only way in and out is the main entrance." I raised my voice to a normal volume. "I'll see you tomorrow, then. So glad you arrived here safely."

His eyes tracked my fingers as they tapped at the very top of the circular door handle twice in a soft, silent movement, and he confirmed my message by tapping on the same location, also twice. We would move at midnight. I stood with my back straight, the veil once again covering my face and my hands neatly overlapping in front of my dress, acting the part of the UnZol King's mate, just as I had promised them I would.

I gave the others the same message as I showed them all to their rooms. Of course, Jenna and Lex shared a room, and she gave me a smile and a wink as she walked in. The warrior in her never backed down from a fight.

I returned to my room and hung my beautiful gown back in the closet. The smooth material glided onto the hanger as easily as it slipped from my skin. If there was one thing I would miss about being the UnZol King's mate, it would be the exquisite taste in clothing. In the mortal world, the outfits would be more than enough to have secured a million mates for the UnZol King. But for me, freedom was worth much more than all the vanities in existence put together. And right now, we had to send a message to the twin gods and to the UnZol

King that we weren't theirs to command. We would make our own decisions and be the rulers of our own destiny.

Slightly before the others, I shadow wove out of my room. I slipped into the darkest mist of the halls, one with the shadows in every corner. We decided to leave in our human forms so we could use our elemental powers if we needed to. I had gotten much better at shadow weaving over the past three years at the Academy. I was the youngest of all naguals to ever shadow weave, and by now I was reaching further and staying in the shadows for far longer than I could before. Every night I had been here I had ventured out to get the lay of this place. I'd gone undetected as I overheard conversations and figured out where they were keeping the relics. Thanks to my intelligence gathering, I had a plan of escape as the time to leave descended upon us.

After counting the guards, their locations and weapons, I knew that we would not go unnoticed as we tried to leave. The Arcana Angels and Zol Demons were too skilled for that to happen. But we had to call their bluff. I expected them not to do their worst, or risk killing me and ruining their precious rite. Our goal instead was to detain them long enough to avoid having the death god return by the time we left. We also needed to harness the power of the relics as we left to protect ourselves from being crucified, and to blast through the spell over the entrance. There was a lot to do, but I knew we could do it.

My first stop would be the Chamber of Pentacles, where the relics were being stored all together at the moment. It was guarded by an ikil. The creature's reptilian eyes were enough to disintegrate you with one look. As a test, I had shadow woven into the chamber several times without removing the relics and had managed to avoid being detected. Just like last time, he didn't even know I was there. I removed each of the six relics one by one, neutralizing the wards on each with one of the black diamonds from my dress and a special spell taught to me by Damian. One by one I slid them inside my satchel without disturbing the creature's slumber.

Then I made my way back to the rooms, stopping at Damian's first. With the slightest tap he knew I was there. I could feel the strength of his deflector spell from the outside. He gave me a curt nod as he left his room as silent as a breeze. I handed him three of the relics in case he needed to use them. He was much more familiar with their magical powers than I was. He put on the Devil's Eye necklace and watched for the Arcana Angels as I guided him down the hall, knocking on the doors of the others. The rest of the unit emerged silently.

As we approached the main entrance, it was almost too easy. We were one step ahead of the guards with every move under Damian's guidance. My breath slowed as I eased my back along the wall, coming up behind an Arcana Angel and striking. I held him in my arms as he fell to the cut of the Stone Mind along his neck. I let his body land with a light thud on the cool tile floor. I shot a glance at Damian; he was busy convincing the guards at the other side of the entrance to let us out the front door with the Snake Tongue, which had the power of persuasion.

"Great job, boys," he told them as they stepped aside to let us pass. "Now lock yourselves in the wine cellar and count all the bottles a hundred times."

They turned aimlessly around and made their way down the hall toward the kitchen where the entrance to the wine cellar was located.

As we approached the gate my excitement grew, knowing we were just about to leave the place unscathed. When my hands touched the smooth metal surface of the door, rain began to pour over our heads. Lightning struck to our right, then our left, and my eyes darted to the others as we tensed in response to the thunder cracking.

"Carly's close. Hurry," Damian whispered.

With my hands still on the massive gate locks, I turned my head and saw Carly walking down the long bridge toward us. "Damian, don't tell me you didn't see that coming."

"I did. She was too fast." He scowled.

Bright, electrical currents rippled from her fingertips as she chanted incantations to summon an electrical storm. I felt the power of the relics in my possession and considered which one I would use against her.

"All you need is me. Let the others go!" I yelled as I turned to face her. I took several steps in her direction, knowing she wouldn't dare hurt me. If she did, she would lose her chance at bringing back the one thing the Dark Zodiac wanted most. As if to demonstrate her power, she called upon a powerful electric field to strike me.

Damian acted quickly, sending an air shield over me as I shadow wove a step to the right. The lightning landed on the ground where I had been standing, leaving a black singe on the earth. Now this bitch was starting to piss me off.

"Give us back the relics and return to the castle. Now," she yelled.

Damian removed a small ivory case from his satchel, the lid engraved with the Cassiopeia constellation for the Obsidian Heart it held within. This was the UnZol King's heart, and he was about to wield its power. Carly shot lightning at him directly, but Jenna reinforced his deflection spell with a powerful wind gust so that the thunder didn't make it through to him. He picked up the Heart, which was an obsidian stone carved into an oval shape.

So that's what a heart as dark as night looks like after years of petrification.

With the Heart in his grasp, all Damian had to do was utter a few words and the largest spiders I had ever seen came crawling out of every crevice and every corner. They charged toward Carly, surrounding her. Her face contorted in a grimace, and she squirmed and screamed as they approached her. This was her worst fear manifested, and that was the power of the Obsidian Heart. We didn't waste any time watching her throw them off of her with spells and fury, almost landing a lightning bolt on herself as she attempted to fight them. She was in a panic, her fear overtaking her and blocking all sense of reason.

I didn't hesitate and shadow wove to the other side of the gate. Zayne had already shadow woven ahead of us and was fumbling with the lock.

"Step back," I told him as I shot a blast of fire at the iron lock in an attempt to melt away the metal and release it. It only weakened but didn't open it. I focused on the hinges and the door began to give way.

When we finally pried the door open, the unit came running through. The others shifted, but I remained in my Zol skin and stayed close to Damian. Their bodies were merely a flash of black as they sprinted past us. My breath came in rapid pants as I ran as fast as I could. It was hard to keep up with the speed of a jaguar. We reached the edge of the forest that surrounded the palace, my legs screaming from the strain of our run. But we were finally outside of the wards that prevented anyone from teleporting in or out of there. I released a long, shaky breath.

"There are more Arcana Angels coming. And other beasts." Damian's jaw was clenched, chin raised.

"Use the Blood Ruby to put us at the eye of a small cyclone. Light this place up with some hurricane winds. They won't get through that," I said as the god's forces closed in on us. I threw the Ruby at Damian, who chanted a spell, and the powerful winds swept the closest demons away and into the wind and rain within. We were in the eye of the hurricane, and we needed the time for everyone to get out of here.

"You guys ready to do the Climb?" Damian asked. The only way into the Underworld was to either die, be sentenced to the prison at Xibalba, or be brought here by the death god. In theory, the unit could Climb back into their bodies at the edge of this forest, where the wards ended, and Damian knew the spell that would carry us through the realm of the spirits and back to the other side.

"Remember, you'll experience every single one of your greatest fears and biggest let-downs in life, a hundred times worse than the first time you had those feelings," he warned us. "Everything will be magnified. You will also learn something about yourself that perhaps you are not ready to know. And that could change your life forever. I am only telling you because you must go through this fully aware of what lies ahead. Are you ready?"

Bjorn shifted to his Zol skin, all two hundred muscular pounds of him stood as a wall at the edge of the forest. What surprised me the most was that his breath was as steady as though he had just strolled through the black forest and hadn't run through it like a jaguar on fire.

"Fuck yeah. I'm ready," Bjorn grunted, a few strands of his thick red hair covering his brow. "Let's do this."

CHAPTER 27

One of the Arcana Angels swept down from over the hurricane winds that surrounded us and toppled Damian over. In two heartbeats Bjorn shifted back into the nagual and he clawed into the Angel's wings from behind, flinging him off of Damian. But Damian had dropped the Ruby, and the winds began dying down. The angel lifted himself off the ground and lunged for the Ruby, but before he could snatch it up Lex tackled him, sending the Ruby flying into the bushes. Lex tried to hold the angel down, but he batted his damaged wings and lifted off the ground.

I heard the call of a dark beast in the distance. A grey mist fell still on the forest floor, where tall, thin black trees grew with their dark branches covered in dense grey-and-black leaves. The forest around the death god's palace was protected by Underworld wolves, Sakti beasts and hexims. These creatures were part of the Zolless armies during the Faellen War. These and many others had found a home here after the battles and were trained for loyalty to the UnZol King.

Jenna shifted into her Zol skin.

"Get out of here, fast. There is something coming for us," Jenna said eyeing the forest, and the others shot each other quick glances, confirming that they heard the same thing I did.

"You're coming with me," I told her.

"And Lex, he's coming too," she said.

Lex shifted back into his Zol skin. "Jenna, you go first," he growled, and by the look in his eye, there would be no arguing with him.

Damian stood next to Lex as I cast fire out at the movement beyond the trees.

"Hurry. Send them fast. I'll be right behind them." I kept channeling fire, keeping whatever was out there at bay.

"We go together." Jenna reached for Lex's hand, and before Lex could protest, Damian cast the Climb spell over them. Their bodies dissipated into the air in a fit of light, fire and dark tendrils that carried their spirits away. They were gone within moments, and I sent a prayer to the stars that they would find their path back to their bodies above.

"Now you." Damian draped the satchel with the other relics over my neck. "All my power must focus in on you at once. The magic of the relics is too powerful and could cause friction as you Climb."

Just then, several large trees were downed by the force coming toward us.

"Two hexims are five clicks away. I'll hold them," I snarled.

"No, you will Climb," he grunted.

Before he could protest any more, I threw the two satchels with the relics at him. He caught them in the air. "Not me. The hexims are too close. The others. Save them," I hissed.

He wanted to resist, but he knew there was no time. The screeching hexim got closer. Large antlers protruded from its skeletal head. Arms and legs twice my size extended from its muscular body, claws the size of large knives lengthening at the ends of bony fingers.

I didn't approach. Instead, I shifted in a few heartbeats and prowled around the creature, snarling. It roared after me, taking steps away from the others. Its large, lion-like mouth opened, revealing razor-sharp teeth, and released a deadly growl that shook the leaves on the trees.

It took a swipe at me and lunged to the right, avoiding my return strike. Another hexim came from around the side of us, and I took a few steps back, positioning myself between them.

Suddenly I sensed that familiar dark movement of two other nagual. I snarled at them. *Fuck, why didn't they Climb?*

Zayne and Bjorn flanked my right and my left. We had the hexims outnumbered, and the odds were in our favor. Damian had five relics in his possession behind me. We could salvage this. Vines sprang from the ground as he wielded the Stone Mind's elemental earth power to create rifts in the rocks surrounding the hexims in an attempt to slow them down. The trees expanded, leafy branches wrapping between them, but all they had to do was swipe their razor-sharp claws to cut through the wood like it was ash.

However, it was useful as a quick distraction, allowing us to take our positions, cornering them. I launched myself at the one closest to me, getting it to swipe and bite at me as I avoided direct contact. Bjorn did the same with the other. And Zayne made his way around to its back unnoticed, lunging for its legs as soon as he got in position and knocking it off balance. The hexim was swift and steadied itself quickly. We exchanged bites and blows, the creature thrashing me against a pile of jagged rocks. I righted myself, my eyes darting to Damian, watching as he wielded the relics against them. Several paces away, more hexims were approaching. With their size and ferocity, they would try to finish us.

I dug my claws in the ground, ready to fight them to the death. Their antlers came crashing down on Zayne, landing with a heavy crunch on his back, sharp claws ripping into his flesh. He healed quickly, but another claw came at him, shredding his nagual coat as black blood spilled in droves from his side. Bjorn wasn't better off, a heavy rip in his face and front legs spilling blood.

A bitter taste entered my mouth as blood spilled from my teeth after the hexim swung at me with a vengeful thrust and slammed me against a tree.

Why are we bleeding like this? We had never bled so much, so fast. Our nagual form was mostly made up of the dark mist. Of shadows and runes. Of the place between physical matter and the ether. We shouldn't be bleeding this much.

I came after the one attacking Zayne and dug my canines deep into its rough, hard flesh. Just as I did another hexim came up and reached for me from behind. Damian blasted it off of me by amplifying his spells with the powers of the relics. Finally, he was getting to know how to handle their magic, and he sent lightning after lightning after lightning bolt after them. They were so close I began to feel the reverberations, my body vibrating from the feeling of the electric charge on my skin and down into my bones.

A sharp pain stung my back, and I yelled out a feral growl in pain as a hexim bit me. Because I was a nagual, the bites of the hexims could not inject me with its savage venom, but they still hurt. Zayne barely responded to my growls in his direction, his body slumped and motionless against the tree. All I could see were claws swiping, fangs lunging from Bjorn, hexims cornering Damian.

I showed him my teeth. *Go!* I snarled at him through the shaman bond.

You must go. Take the relics and go. Don't worry about me. They won't kill me. Take the others and Climb. Right now.

I'm not going anywhere. Plus you don't know how to cast the Climb spell. And Bjorn and Zayne won't make the Climb. Not as they are. Their bodies need to heal first.

Damian fumbled with the relics, considering which to use next. These relics preyed on the fragility of a society and the heart of a complex consciousness. They were practically useless on hexims that only cared about bringing de-struction and chaos. They didn't have fears. They didn't tend to young or live in villages. They feasted off the pain they inflicted, the devastation they caused and the blood of their prey.

I looked around at the four hexims that we were now fighting, my breath coming in heavy pants and my heart pounding in my chest. Zayne would be torn into; the next swipe of the hexim's claws would split him open. Just as that thought entered my mind, I lunged for the arm that reached for him, and then it happened. A deadly blow to his side. His blood splattered everywhere.

Bjorn was the only one of us truly holding them off. I watched him take one of them down, knocking it to the ground with a fierce grip and pinching its neck until the massive antlered creature stopped resisting. I turned my attention back to Zayne, dodging a swipe from a hexim as I did. Zayne was on the ground a few feet from me, his breathing slowed. I searched his green jaguar eyes. A pained stare shot back at me just as I was thrown into another set of jagged rocks, my skull banging on a pointed edge, ringing sounding in my ears.

Go, Damian. Now. I could barely make out the words I sent to Damian through the bond, but he just had to listen and get those relics out of here.

His hands moved quickly, gripping onto every bit of magic he could garner from the air that surrounded us. He cast three shield wards of protection, conjuring a transparent blue shield in front of us, the slicing claws of the hexims unable to get through. *If we could just take the other three hexims down, we could heal quickly and then make the Climb out of the Underworld.*

Four more hexims could be seen approaching from the south of us, two more from the east. Several other dark shapes were approaching from the dark mist behind us, and my heart caught in my throat.

We need to run.

I was searching for an escape when I felt the fiercest blow from my right side. With a swift movement, the hexim tore through Damian's magical shield, and three elongated claws etched along my rib cage. Black blood spilled faster than I could heal. I let out a soft growl before falling to the ground with a heavy thud. My breath hitched. There wasn't enough air. My vision blurred. I was dizzy.

"You aren't running anywhere. Instead, you will bow." Vucub-Cane appeared before us, as though he had been standing there the entire time. "You do realize that this is my Underworld? I know of every transgression in my realm. I don't need to be told, by anyone. I can feel the dishonesty, the deceit. It courses through my being as though you were pulling at my veins with a string. There is no greater power in my Underworld. There is no way to escape me. Just as I allowed Jenna and Lex to leave, I may decide to allow you to live. You're bleeding pretty badly."

He scanned my body, then shifted his eyes to Bjorn, his gaze lingering. Then his eyes fell on Damian, whose brows were creased with frustration. As he took us all in, his creatures of the Underworld still surrounded us, a semicircle of monsters panting and releasing low growls as they awaited his command.

"Fate will guide the others back here. When the time is right. And as for you." The god stepped closer to me, hovering over my limp body as I was bleeding out.

I stole a glance at Bjorn; he was also bleeding out. Zayne looked dead. Damian was the only one of us standing, his brow creasing at the sight of the two fallen warriors.

"Not sure if you'll be dancing at your wedding, seeing as how deep those cuts are. Now don't try and leave here again," Vucub-Cane warned.

CHAPTER 28

The god began to walk away. I wasn't sure if I saw him leave, or if he disappeared before my eyes. I knew the gods were powerful, but I realized just then that I had no idea how truly powerful they were. My eyes continued to blur, and my awareness was slipping. I looked out through hazy eyes to see if the creatures of death had retreated. All I saw was Damian rushing over to me. I couldn't exactly tell what he was doing, but it felt like he was trying to cast healing spells.

"Hang on, Sasha. Hang on." A sense of urgency laced his faraway voice.

I didn't want to cling to his voice, my soul too weak to grip on. "I'm going to rest," I whispered.

The warmth of his hand hovered over my bleeding wound. "The death god is not allowing you to heal." The dried black leaves that covered the ground crackled under his feet as he rushed over to Bjorn. "He's the same. He's not healing."

Damian reached in the satchel where the relics still were, and he pulled out the Snake Tongue. I closed my eyes and imagined myself back in Trent's arms for comfort. Then I remember what he'd done, and a dim fire rose in my chest. I didn't have the energy for any more anger toward him than that.

Damian returned to my side and said, "Darkness reborn, serve the Zol as one."

I repeated the mantra in my mind after him. My thoughts slowed, stopped, then started again. Slowly and painfully. *Who am I serving? That fucking death god or the other asshole death god? Or am I serving the people of Zol Stria? If I'm serving the Zol, then this whole concept of the nagual answering to the gods, or even the Zol Council, isn't working. I may no longer be inside Xibalba, but I am inside a prison.* Words from the sphinx's riddle came back to me. *"A slave I have been and shall remain."*

They own us. We are theirs to command and this whole situation, just isn't going to work for me. I want to be free or dead. So, he might as well kill me.

"He almost did kill you. Hang on, Sashita," Damian grunted as he worked on my injuries. My eyes flickered open at his voice, and then my gaze landed on Bjorn, who was taking shallow breaths. His eyes were closed.

Go help the others. Please.

Bjorn was the great warrior nagual. His fighting in the arena had earned him the top place among us. And he was now even closer to death than I was. Damian glanced over at him while still hovering the Snake Tongue over my side. I had stopped feeling the warm blood flowing out of me and managed to lift my head enough to see that the three long slashes along my side were beginning to close, just very slowly.

So... slowly.

Damian darted up and went over to Bjorn, speaking the same incantations as he had over me, and he managed to stop the blood. Bjorn just looked so weak lying there, the life sucked out of him.

I fought to keep my mind in this world, not allowing it to drift as it wanted to. Some time passed, I wasn't sure how much, and Damian said to me, "Can you shift to your Zol skin? Do you have the strength? We've got to get you back to the palace so they can heal you properly. The death god wants you weak and wounded, otherwise he would have healed you before leaving. He also would have taken the relics with him if he believed any of us could leave. But you can't leave the Underworld with how hurt you are. You and Bjorn won't make the Climb."

I managed to shake my head slightly in protest.

"Quite literally, it appears he wants you crawling back to him."

Then you leave. Take the relics. Get them out of here and don't look back.

"Not this time, Sasha. I won't leave you," he said. There were centuries of feeling in those words, and I was too weak to argue. "I need to get you back to the palace. You and Bjorn won't make it there without me. I need to find that Blood Ruby." His eyes scanned the bushes where it had fallen. "With it, I should be able to cast enough wind energy to carry you to the palace. Plus, I figure that even if I try to leave the Underworld, the death god will come back and sever my head. He left me with these relics so I could make the trip back. He knows exactly what he's doing. Now, are you strong enough to shift?"

I was so tired, so hurt, so beaten and broken that the only thing I could do was take in a shaky breath and sob inside my soul.

"Be strong, Sasha. I can feel your hurt. But you can't give up. If you die, if you stop fighting, you lose all your chances. You can only fight if you're alive." This coming from a man who had given up every fight after the love of his life, and the mother of his unborn child, had died. He was fighting for me right now, after decades of giving up on me. Of giving up on himself. If he was willing to fight for me, as much as it hurt, as much as I hated the idea of bowing to anyone and allowing any god to have complete domination and control over my destiny, I had to hate it enough to fight to change it. Even if I refused to give the god what he wanted and mate the UnZol King, staying here and giving up would mean that future generations of nagual would continue to be servants of the gods. Assassins for their cause and theirs to command. If it took the rest of my centuries in this world, being alive would give me the chance to find a way to break the chains that bound us to them.

My mind began to come back to me. Clear, cohesive thoughts began to form, and I remembered how to shift. I pulled in the darkness; there was so much of it here. I drew from the strength of the ancients, those souls that traveled in this Underworld, floating in the mist around me. The forgotten and the broken. The unforgiven and the damned. The mist was rich with their darkness, and the shadows were fuel for my transformation.

Let's rip off the Band-Aid. The quicker I shifted, the less painful it would be. In several heartbeats I was a naked woman, lying on the floor of a cold forest, the wounds of the slashes still very fresh on my side. They would be leaving a scar.

Dark hairs fell around my face as I hauled myself from the ground to my elbows and observed the many sharp, black-and-grey rocks underneath my palms. My fingers curled around them, the uneven edges piercing my soft flesh. I could taste the metallic tang of blood that dripped from my mouth onto the dark ground, a small crimson pool forming. It was my blood and not the blood of those monsters. Every part of my body ached as the black blood of my jaguar smeared onto my legs and torso as I continued to lift myself up to my knees.

My eyes lifted to where Zayne's body remained lifeless against a black forest tree. His jaguar form faded right before my eyes into the pale, lifeless skin of a male. My instincts were to rush toward him, but my body wouldn't respond.

"You've lost too much blood. Put this on, then you'll have to sit and rest. We will make our way back tomorrow." Damian gave me a shirt and pants from the satchel he carried and handed the other to Bjorn, who was in a similar state.

"What of Zayne?" I asked, my voice shaking.

He shook his head, his bearded face wretched with sorrow. Stones dropped inside my chest. My mentor. My friend. Gone.

"I'm so sorry... I'm so sorry..." I kept repeating. A more experienced fighter would have saved him. A better warrior would never have let this happen.

"I am too," Damian said.

I tried to move, but a fiery pain shot from every nerve in my body.

Damian created a sphere of light, empty on the inside so that it looked like a golden bubble floating just above his hand. He went to Zayne and kneeled, the clear orb glowing over his body. Misty tendrils shed from his still flesh. Damian seemed to try to speak, but nothing left his throat. He coughed and sighed, then started again.

"*Life bound by darkness.*
Duty bound by honor.
Death bound by light.
Now your FaeSource returns to the eye of the Mother.
Truth be your guide in the endless night."

As Damian spoke, Zayne's elemental light lifted from his body, which lay flat upon the ground, covered with the leaves of the earth and clothed in a black shirt and pants that Damian had brought for the shifters. I didn't even notice when Damian put on his clothes, my head a hazy fog.

"Darkness reborn, serve the Zol as one," Bjorn said, and I repeated the words, my eyes opening wide as his gaze met mine. I dragged my body over to his side and wrapped an arm around his back as he leaned against me. He was badly injured but far from beaten. We would both survive this to fight another day.

"We got our asses kicked," he groaned as he placed a hand over his ribs. From the slight grimace on his face, I could tell several ribs must have been broken.

"We did. At the hands of the god who created us. This is how he treats the children who disobey him," I said.

"And now we have to go back there," he said, his eyes scanning the area for some other escape. Some other way out. Yet, as much as we went over it on that cold, dark forest floor, we couldn't find an option that left us coming out of there alive.

"We will go back and heal. Recover. And I will return for the rite." That last word stung as it left my mouth.

"And we will find another way out," Bjorn grumbled as I placed my head on his shoulder.

CHAPTER 29

T he return to the obsidian palace began during the brightest part of the day and ended as the suns had dimmed, wrapping us under the cover of darkness. Damian used the Blood Ruby to carry us with the relic's air magic. But we had to go slowly, because every bump and jostle caused sharp pains to shoot through our bodies and release blood from our still-open wounds. We would not begin to heal until we reached the palace and the death god granted us some relief.

I couldn't hold my head upright. Sweaty black strands of hair clung to my cheek and neck, falling into my eyes and making them itch, and I didn't have the energy to lift my hands to wipe the strands away. Feeling weak like this reminded me of how my mind had worked before I had ever shifted, when I was all human, fighting my fears and against the dark thoughts that tormented me in the dark of night and light of day. Instead of feeding off the shadows, like I had learned to do over the past few years, my mind drifted between conscious and unconscious thoughts. All my barriers and deflector spells were down. The oddly familiar and maddening voices that had once plagued me returned as my thoughts became blurry and tormented.

It's all my fault that Zayne, the master nagual warrior, returned to the Mother way too soon. He had hundreds of years left.

This one marring thought began to repeat in my mind, and other dark thoughts followed. I was the reason they were captured in the first place. I was the one who had come up with the plan to leave. I was the one who had insisted everyone escape with me.

It's all my fault.

I couldn't stop thinking of Zayne, and, with this one dark thought, the shadows that once fueled me began to attack me. High-pitched screeches of the Underworld vibrated in my head as nails felt like they were being drilled into my skull. My arms and legs felt itchy, my clothes too tight as sweat drenched my hair, and it felt sticky in my palms. My neck wasn't strong enough to hold up my head, and I thrashed as my eyes rolled backward. The dark shadows were no longer feeding me, they began to feed off of me. I was drifting to sleep and into a dream...

I was in the middle of the black forest, standing alone. My hair was dry and so were my clothes, my wounds had healed but blood stained my hands and shirt. Directly in front of me was Zayne's body, laying still and pale, a single drop of blood spilling from his mouth. I looked down at the blood covering my fingers and palms, then I ran my hands into my hair, clutching and pulling at the strands. I screamed at the top of my lungs, an agonizing, fitful scream, falling to my knees as the painful cry left my throat. Hot tears spilled down my cheeks as I wept at his side.

Dark, misty tendrils curled around me. It was a distantly familiar mist, and it filled me with a comforting emotion. It gently swept against my cheek and chin, over my shoulders, and curled around my waist.

"This doesn't have to keep happening. You don't have to watch your family die."

The voice startled me. I thought I was alone in this realm of complete darkness, this place in my mind between reality and death. I released my hands from my hair and shifted my gaze in front of me.

There stood the UnZol King, his fine shirt resting softly against the contrast of the firm lines of his muscles. A tattoo appeared around his neck, which looked like it probably continued underneath the cream-colored shirt he was wearing. His hair was an inky black that matched his black beard. Long strands fell to his shoulders, accenting his black eyes.

"Ok, first of all, what is your name?" I scoffed. "UnZol King? Come on. I can't keep calling you that. Why does everyone call you that?"

"It has a ring to it. Anyway, I like it." His lips curled into a smile. "My name is Balastar Ramon del Castillo. You used to call me Star."

Something about the name was familiar, like a scent or a taste I hadn't experienced in a very long time.

"Ok, Star." I drew out each syllable. "Why are you doing this?"

"You can't run from your fate. I am your destiny," he said, and I stared into his eyes but saw nothing but a black hole where his soul should be.

"I should be able to choose my own destiny. I don't want to be forced to do anything. Zayne would never have wanted to die just so I could become your property. I don't belong to you, or anyone!" I planted myself on my two feet and stood, the pain of the wounds a faint memory stinging at my side.

"You are wrong, Sasha. You do belong to me. You belong to the death gods who created you, you belong to your destiny, and you will become my mate." His face was passive and impossible to read.

"You're right." I controlled my breathing, calmed my fire. "I will mate with you, but only to save the others. You know, for the briefest moment, I thought there was more to you. I thought there could be a chance that some of the stories about you weren't true. That you were, in fact, the voice of those who were broken and forgotten. But instead, you're a monster."

He stepped closer, and I held my ground. I would not back away from him. I would not stand here afraid. I would face him head on until my death.

But his approach was subtle, his lips soft and his eyes focused with longing on my mouth. "You loved me once, Sasha. Remember who you truly are."

"I could never love you."

I gritted my teeth as he lightly swept his hand over my side, soothing the pain that shot through me. His mouth was close enough to kiss mine, my traitorous lips quivering with the desire to feel his next to them. I didn't know who I was anymore. I was being swept away, lifted outside of my body, and floating above as I watched the body I was in release herself to him. She brought her hand to his jaw and held his face, looking into his eyes as though she was in love with him.

"There you are. I knew you were in there," he told her, his head tilting toward her.

"No!" I yelled. "That's not me."

He had the nerve to look up to where my essence was floating above the two of us, inside the same golden orb I'd seen Zayne drift into. My FaeSource had been removed, and now I was looking down at what, the me that was before?

I was still so dizzy; this must be just a bad dream. I closed my eyes and tried to look away, hoping that when I opened them again, he would be gone. This whole scene couldn't be happening. But when I closed my eyes, I felt a warmth on my lips. I felt a tender, loving touch that rose desire from deep within me. My eyes fluttered open, again hoping I was wrong. Hoping that now the dream would end. Instead, I saw them still beneath me. His hands caressed her back down to her waist, gripping it tightly with longing. She returned his kiss, her mouth opening to him, her hands against his firm chest, their embrace fiery with passion and heat.

Stars, help me.

He kissed her again, and again. His hand at the back of her head, his fingers woven between the long, thick strands of her hair. He pulled away and ran his thumb softly against her bottom lip as she gave him a tender smile.

"Sasha, this is who you are. All you have to do is remember." Warmth pooled in my center when he said this; I felt his every touch from up here in the golden orb. Even though I couldn't resist him, I knew that deep down a part of me truly didn't want to.

Suddenly, the rocking movement I had become accustomed to stopped. My eyes opened, and I looked at the palace doors. I was awake, and we had arrived.

CHAPTER 30

M y skin bristled as we crossed the heavy doors at the entrance to the death god's palace. The walls seemed to close in on us as we approached. I looked down at my side, which was still bleeding. My hands were restrained with black vines, as were my legs. I looked over at Damian.

"I tried to wake you," Damian said. "You were having a nightmare. Yelling and thrashing about. I had to restrain you because I didn't want you to hurt yourself. You have a fever. That wound is severely infected. You need a healer right now."

I checked under the soaked bandage and saw wet blood at the center, a ring of dried blood around yellow-and-blue pus.

As we entered the anteroom, the walls and shapes inside the palace were blurry. It felt as though I was both awake and sleeping, and my mind drifted back to the goat shed at my aunt's home in the mountains where I had hidden as a child. I had wrapped myself in a blanket and curled my knees into my chest to hide from my parents.

I was being moved. Damian had me in his arms and was setting me down on a stretcher held by two Zol Demons. The movement snapped me out of my dream and brought me back to this painful realty. I sensed the presence of the death god; his energy vibrated at a much different level than any Fae or human. I opened my eyes to slits and saw him standing several paces away, flanked by his Arcana Angel guards. I couldn't see them, but I could make out their outlines and felt their cold stares on my bloodied body.

"Your Grace, we are at your mercy," Damian said, holding out the satchel with the relics, and an Arcana Angel stepped forward, retrieved them and walked away.

The death god stood over me, and I saw his white hair contrast with his deep golden skin. Although I couldn't see his expression, I guessed it was one of deep satisfaction. "Bring her to the healer at the west wing," was all he said, and then he was gone.

My eyes closed, and I no longer felt his vast, unrestrained power consuming all the space in the room.

The Zol healers were gentle; four of them tended to Bjorn and me. They cast healing magic and applied an ointment that soothed the pain instantly.

"The infection has taken a strong hold. So strong that your ability to heal will be slowed to the rate of a human's until we can clear the infection. It is an infection of the soul, not just the body. You must make peace with your path. It is the only way to clear the infection. Here, drink this." The Zol healer handed me a sleeping draft that I swiftly drank down. The taste was bitter and made my mouth feel tart. "This will help so we can work on the wound. You won't feel any pain."

I shifted my gaze to Bjorn. The color had returned to his face, and his healer didn't have the same concerned look that mine had.

"He's healing faster because he has made peace with his path. You haven't," my healer said.

"Well, he doesn't have to mate with a monster, after all," I mumbled.

"You're going to be all right," Damian said, stepping out of the shadows behind the healer.

"I know." I nodded, but a smile refused to surface. Zayne was gone, and there were a thousand reasons why I couldn't bear it.

"We need to keep working on her. Please, leave us," I heard the healer say to Damian, just as everything faded to black.

I wasn't sure how much time had passed, but I found myself back in my room. The curtains were closed, and the room was dark. I reached down to my side and felt a bandage in place, the muslin material wrapped entirely around my torso. My eyes adjusted, and although things were still blurry, I was able to make out some shapes in the darkness. I tried to pull in the shadows to draw power from the dark energy around me, but it wasn't working. I felt as though I had no power or abilities, as though I was not a nagual. I closed my eyes. Maybe tomorrow I'd feel stronger.

The next time I opened my eyes it was to the sound of the door opening and a healer entering.

"You're awake," she said, her voice soft under her satin brown hood. "I've been checking on you for three days. You stirred in your sleep. You chanted in the ancient tongue. What must you have seen to make you so restless, I wonder?" She bustled out of the room, and my Fae hearing was starting to return, because I could hear her telling someone about me. The pink-haired Fae healer quickly returned and continued to check me, her bright pink wings fluttering at her back.

"Are you from House Sagittarius?" I said, my throat rough like sandpaper. I was always fascinated to learn where each of the Fae I met were from. The differences between them could range from striking to subtle, depending on their ancestry, from fingernails to wings, teeth to hair, limbs and heights. The Zol healer's features were so strong; she was as far away from human as any Fae I had ever seen.

"Yes. I serve the Dark Zodiac, and you will be my queen soon. I am honored to serve you," she said.

"Why? Why would you be honored to serve me?" I asked.

"Because the Zol Council has forgotten who we are. We are more than just the Fae that either live by the light or feed from the dark. There are shades of grey, and those in the grey are being lumped into those being hunted, those being persecuted for not abiding by the old doctrines. The ruling class's way of doing things has been a way of oppression, a way of privilege through force. There are the Fae with means, and those without." She checked my bandage and applied more of the thick yellow ointment so tenderly that I barely felt her touch. She kept pink eyes focused on my wound as she continued, "We believe the Half-Fae should live among us and not in hiding. We don't need to be separate from humans, but we should unite with them. This is what the Dark Zodiac is fighting for." Her voice was steady, calm and sincere. Although her skin glowed and her hair fell softly around her face, she had a hardness to her tongue that only came with having fought personal battles with the Zol Council.

"How do you know they aren't lying to you?" I asked.

She scoffed. "Lying. Ha." Her laugh was dry and absent of humor. She narrowed her eyes as she examined my wound. "My firstborn child was taken by House Sagittarius when he was six years old, and I have not seen him since. They don't take all the firstborns. Only the ones like mine. Our blood is magical and can enhance the powers of others if they drink it. They either killed him and fed from him, or they slowly fed from him every day. "

Her eyes were as full of anger as I had ever seen in a female.

"He was summoned to the House for the ritual where he would be handed over, and I refused to take him. I ran and they found me. Someone told them where I was hiding. They ripped my sweet boy from my arms and left me to die. But I am a healer. So, I healed myself, and when I heard that the god Vucub-Cane needed a healer, I came here. No one wants to work for Xibalba, but I had to leave Zol Stria." She released a sigh and scrunched her lips to the side. "The wound is healing like a human's wound. If it keeps on like this, you won't be able to walk during the rite."

"Why am I not healing?"

She shrugged her shoulders. "Your wound was really infected. The hexim's venom is a deadly sickness for Fae. It renders some of our abilities numb, including our ability to heal. If your shaman didn't get you back here when he did, you would have died." She quickly looked away and began organizing her supplies.

I took her wrist in my hand and let heat rise to the surface. "What aren't you telling me?"

"Zol help me." She released a heavy sigh. "Vucub-Cane wants some insurance. He doesn't want you to run again, so he has spun a spell to keep you wounded until the rite."

I opened my hand, releasing her wrist. Her first-degree burns from my hold healed instantly. This was the second time I had almost died. A shuddering chill coursed down my spine. "Where is Damian?" I asked.

She looked over to the doorway, where he was standing. I hadn't sensed him approach.

"Hey. You're looking much better," he said.

"Don't fucking lie." I ran a hand through my sticky, knotted hair. It hadn't been brushed.

"You're right. You still look like shit, but a little less like shit than you did three days ago." He chuckled.

I caught sight of an Arcana Angel standing just outside the door, his grey wings bristling ever so slightly.

"You've got a full-time guard assigned," he said, catching the questioning look in my eye.

"I suppose I do."

"Here, take this," the healer said. "It's just something to help with the inflammation and the pain. The rite is just a few days away. I expect your healing abilities to return soon."

I raised the small cup like it was a shot and smirked as I drank it down. The healer left, and Damian sat in the chair at my side.

"How's Bjorn?" I asked. He had to be ok. I couldn't lose anyone else.

"He's fine. It seems he's healing faster than you are, but only because your wounds were much more infected than his were."

"Can I see him?" "Yes, soon enough."

"Lex and Jenna? Did they make it?" *Please tell me they made it.*

"Their FaeSources are strong. They are both together, even stronger as cardinal signs."

"That's right. They are cardinal signs, the signs of new beginnings."

"Exactly. It helped propel them past the Barren Lands of Lost Time and the Boneyard of Confused Suffering. Being a cardinal sign meant they could hang on to that deeper aspect of themselves, that belief they were on the path to start again. And that was enough to get them through the Climb to the other side."

"Thank the stars. Otherwise, their souls would have returned to Xibalba for eternal agony." Never to return in any incarnation. "What about Eliana?"

"I gave her guard an elixir he wanted in exchange for him allowing untrace-able amounts of dark energy to enter the room whenever he brought her food. I'm sure Vucub-Cane knows what we're up to. It is his passive way of giving you something you want. This will keep her stable, for a while longer." His eyes shifted, as though he didn't like any of this either. Over the past few years, he had grown close to us. We had become one unit.

"Tell them I will only do this if they also release Eliana."

Damian nodded. "I will."

"And give Zayne a proper burial," I said softly, the words felt like broken glass as they left my throat.

"I insisted on that when we arrived. We will give him a hero's funeral at the rite."

CHAPTER 31

"Well, for what it's worth, I'm glad you're here," I said. "Whatever happens, I want you to know that I'm glad I found you and I, well... I appreciate you. I'm glad you're my shaman and even though it can be hard to tell sometimes, I think you're a good person." After losing Zayne so suddenly, I didn't want anything to go left unsaid. Damian needed to know how I felt about him.

"Don't go getting all sentimental. I'm going to be around for a while longer. I'm not going anywhere." He wore a smug look.

"Yeah, you will. But you are important to me, and I just need to say it." After all that had happened, he hadn't disappeared again. He'd stayed by my side, fighting with me as a true confidant only could.

"Sure. Ok, I'll say it, too. You're important to me." He stood close to my bed, his broad shoulders pulled back, his jaw set and his golden eyes glimmering. He was being sincere, and it was weird.

I began to chuckle, then I sputtered out a loud laugh that had me covering my mouth. I laughed so hard I closed my eyes and cocked my head back, gripping my side from the pain the laughing brought on. But it was so worth it. I peeked at him while I was laughing and he had shifted on his feet, a side of his mouth lifted. He began to laugh nervously.

"What? What is it you're laughing at?"

"I got you to say it. I got the big, mysterious, unemotionally attached Shaman Damian Burgos to say I'm important to him. I have to tell the others I won the bet," I said between chuckles.

"Ha, ha. So that's why you got all sappy on me? Just to win a bet?" he asked incredulously.

"Yeah, pretty much. They bet me that you didn't care about anyone but yourself, and I bet that you did. Today, I won."

"Lucky you," he said, and he didn't seem as annoyed as I had hoped he would be.

"Yep. Lucky me." I released a ragged breath; all that laughing had drained my energy. My eyes drifted out of the window. A tropical view was on display. It was one of the illusion spells they had in this palace, the creation of false views of beautiful locations. I guessed it must be somewhere in Hawaii or the South Pacific, or perhaps the tropical lands found in the House of Cancer. Palm trees rustled in a sea breeze, and the waves sparkled like diamonds in the midday sun.

"So, what do you think about this battle between the Dark Zodiac and Zol Stria? I've got Carly and the healer both telling me they're all for the Dark Zodiac uprising. They want the UnZol King to return to command his Zolless armies again." I explained to Damian what they had told me and how they saw the return of the UnZol King as their chance to come out of the shadows and unite with the rest of Zol Stria.

He didn't seem surprised by this. "Of course, there have always been stories," he said. "Fae who have gone missing. The custom of taking the firstborn on their sixth birthday. Then there was the abuse of power. The drugs being pumped into the hands of the lesser-born, keeping them hooked while the Vicars exploited them. Or the Fae at casinos and bars being sent to Xibalba for crimes that never got explained completely. There are so many layers of lies to sift through. And of course, there was what happened with Ixia. How everything she did went unchecked, and they welcomed her back so easily." His gaze followed my distant stare out the window.

"And there's the intolerable Vicars and Council members who have grown even more pompous and arrogant over the years since I disappeared," he continued. "But I was too self-absorbed to even care or pay attention. Now I can see where this all stems from. The UnZol King does make some bit of sense. They say that the enemy of my enemy is my friend. If we join with the Dark Zodiac, we will have more of those that can help me find and kill Ixia. Now that they've accepted her back at the Council and we are on the run, it makes it very hard for me to even come near her. So, for my own selfish reasons, I would be open to an alliance." He turned to me and angled his head. "But my stakes aren't as high as yours. No one is asking me to be the mate of the deadliest and most powerful Fae to have ever existed. Sasha, this is your life we're talking about." His eyes narrowed on me, and my breath hitched.

"It just seems so extreme. What about Solana? She's an evil bitch. I'm still pissed at her for turning Trent and taking his heart from me." I shuddered at the sting these words left my mouth.

"As far as I see it, Trent's heart was never yours. He was in your life for a reason and exactly at a time when you needed him. But the stars have you both on different paths."

"So, are you saying that the UnZol King is my path? That the stars actually want this for me?" I shook my head.

"I have to think they do. In the six thousand years of cihuatl rituals, they have never been wrong."

"What if it was rigged? What if there was some magic spell done to alter that vision? At this point, anything is possible, isn't it?" I asked.

"The kind of magic needed to alter the cihuatl vision doesn't exist." He seemed so certain of this. "And you are his Zol Mate, right? Vucub-Cane confirmed this?"

"Yes, he did." I nodded slowly.

"Then this part is true. Vucub-Cane already has all six relics, which are the ones we saw in the vision. And the rite is in just a few days." He breathed in heavily, his chest lifting. "Everything is lining up as though the vision is true."

My throat tightened. "I don't want to be his mate. I don't want to be forced to do anything."

"I know." He dropped down in the chair beside me. "Yet here we are. I wish there was another way." His eyes locked with mine, and I knew he was out of ideas. So was I.

"Ok, so walk me through this mating ritual? What happens, exactly? I mean, he isn't even a physical being. How am I supposed to marry a ghost?"

Damian laughed.

"That's not funny!"

He kept laughing. "Yeah. Yeah, you're right. It's not funny." He kept chuckling. "Ok, so in modern history we haven't brought anyone back, but this is an ancient ritual, said to have been performed and perfected over many centuries before the creation of the twelve Houses of Zol Stria. In those years, gods would go into their great sleep and return under the guidance of the Zol Sen. Let's say a fair and balanced god was needed, then the Libra constellation would be channeled to awaken Thoth, the Egyptian god of equilibrium, in order to restore order. Many say that the loss of this practice is why our world is spiraling to chaos."

"And so, what happens at the ritual?" I insisted.

"Pretty much it will happen just like you saw in the vision. Having the six relics and you present will be enough for him to take physical form. Once you come into contact with him for the first time, you should feel the mating bond take hold. You will not be able to resist the bond between you."

"Is it like our bond? Where you can speak to me in my jaguar form?"

"Yes, it's very much like that." His eyes shifted.

"What? There's something you're not telling me." I sat upright in my bed.

"No, it's nothing."

"I know you. I can tell it's not nothing."

He scratched the hair of his beard. "It's just, our bond will be gone. It will be replaced with his."

My eyes opened wide, and my chest tightened. I wasn't expecting that. I released a breath. "Well, that sucks."

"It does.." He said, then he gave me a half-smile. "Then again, maybe now I'll finally have some peace."

"Well then, you're welcome." I rolled my eyes and chuckled.

CHAPTER 32

Tonight, the full moon was in Aquarius, and the rite was upon me. The Oscuri Elf helped me dress in the fine black gossamer gown that fell like a soft breeze over my skin. As she used her elegant fingers to clasp the buckles, she slowly lifted her grey eyes to meet mine.

"You look beautiful." Her voice was gentle.

"I'm nervous."

"Don't be nervous. You are doing a great service for so many of us. We need you, more than you can imagine. You will be the one to set us free." Her voice shook with emotion, and her fingers began to tremble. I wrapped my hands around hers. All I could do was nod my head. I knew that so many believed that this was the right thing to do, but it went against everything I thought about love. I would be mated to a man I hadn't even fallen in love with. A man I knew nothing about.

"Thank you, Senai." I turned from her to face the mirror and dropped the veil over my eyes. Carly was waiting for me at the doorway, and together we left for the ceremony.

We arrived sometime later at the great pyramid of the Underworld. It was in the center of Xibalba, and it was a pyramid made of pure obsidian stone. There were golden carvings for each of the zodiac constellations all over the pyramid, making it look like a part of the night sky had found its place right here in the Underworld.

We teleported inside a palace tent where I was told to wait until we were called. I could hear many voices outside. The Dark Zodiac had gathered in great numbers here to watch the ceremony unfold, and they were granted access to only this part of the Underworld just to watch the ceremony take place. I peeked out of the side of the tent to observe those in attendance, and I was surprised at what I saw. I expected to see only ruthless monsters, gangsters and killers, but instead I saw farmers. Families. Fae of every age and size. Warriors and sword-wielders, seamstresses and healers and so many others. They had hopeful expressions, and the energy was light and bouncy.

Damian entered the tent, his face expressionless.

Carly spoke first. "Thank you, Damian. For..." She waved her hand at me. "For bringing her and the relics back here."

Damian nodded, his eyes narrowed slightly.

A moment later Eliana came into the tent. Her eyes widened as she stared at me in my gown and the elaborate decor of my tent. "They finally let me out of there," she joked, pulling a long strand of her dark hair behind her ear. She had changed into jeans, a T-shirt and sneakers.

"Thank Zol," I said, placing my hands on her shoulders and giving her a kiss on the cheek. She returned the kiss.

A Zol Demon pulled open the tent door and stood at the entrance. "It is time. The god Vucub-Cane awaits."

"Well. Then let's go meet my Zol Mate."

It was just like the vision, but I was seeing it through my own eyes. I couldn't believe I was here, in the same exact situation I had fought with my life to avoid. A situation that Zayne had given his life to avoid.

My black heels clicked with every step they climbed, and I lifted my head to see what awaited me at the very top. The crowd around us hushed as I made my way up, followed by Carly just a few steps behind. My eyes lifted to the platform at the top, and there stood the god Vucub-Cane along with the Zol Sen in the black-hooded cloak. His Arcana Angel guards circled overhead. Grey-and-black clouds were scattered across the sky, along with orange-and-crimson light from the tiny suns high in the distant rock above.

When I reached the top, the corner of the death god's eyes gave away a faint glimmer of satisfaction in his otherwise expressionless face. The Zol Sen read from ancient scripture as Carly placed the relics on me. The Blood Ruby was slid onto my finger, the belt with the Stone Mind in its sheath was wrapped around my dress, the Devil's Eye was placed around my neck and the Blade Bone was a sword placed on the table next to the Snake Tongue and the Obsidian Heart. As soon as the items were placed on me, a cold breeze began to swirl around us. Its cold chill shuddered down my spine and blew the hood off the Zol Sen's cloak, revealing her golden hair and fair skin.

Carly stepped forward, as though she either expected this to happen or had decided that the show must go on. She began to say an incantation, and, although I couldn't understand the words, the cold breeze settled. All became still, and the UnZol King appeared before us.

A pulsing, dark power threaded through me unlike anything I had ever felt. The crowd fell completely silent at the sight of him, and the god Vucub-Cane approached us both.

"The stars write the path," he said. "You were once, and you are again."

Carly stood behind the table with the relics and faced us, holding her arms wide as the god channeled dark power from the relics. He swept his hand forward, and the relics glowed crimson. He pulled their magic, along with a power coming from deep inside of me, into the UnZol King. He filled him with the dark mist that curled around him. Tendrils of shadow and mist filled every crevice of his being until he was completely covered in it. When he was filled, the black eyes of a perfectly beautiful face opened. His features were almost feline. Animal and man. Dark hair fell softly around his thick eyebrows, his jaw tight and set.

My eyes locked with his, and I couldn't stop looking at him. My heart began to beat so loudly in my chest that I felt it may burst out of it.

He smiled a gentle, familiar smile that revealed a dimple on the left side, and a memory of that dimple flashed in my mind. It was an image so clear that I wanted to run my hand along his jaw and pull him toward me.

"I'm back, Sasha. We are one, again," he said, and held out his hand.

I wanted to take it so badly that I began to reach for him, then I pulled my hand back, fidgeting with my fingers.

"You must make contact, Sasha. To begin the creation of the bond," Carly said. In the days before the rite Carly had told me where I should stand and exactly what I needed to do. She drilled it into me that my role was critical to the UnZol King's return because I was his anchor to this world. But that wasn't enough of a motivator for me to carry through with this. The fact that I was his anchor didn't make my heart pure, like it needed to be for this to work.

I scanned the top of the pyramid. Everyone was looking at us. I had forgotten I was even up here; I had gotten carried away in my thoughts and in the moment.

The UnZol King reached for me again, and I considered taking the Stone Mind out of its sheath at my side and stabbing him in the heart. But the death god was standing right there, and my unit and I would likely be tortured with a slow and painful death if I disobeyed. *No, better stick to the plan.*

I placed my hand in his, and the moment I did, memories coursed through me. It was as though every single memory of my past life awoke and flowed through my mind. We were deeply, madly in love those many centuries ago. He looked at me, his eyes full of longing, and I could tell how deeply he had missed me. I could feel it. My thoughts and desires were not a compulsion, like when I was glamoured by Grange. Instead, my mind was awake, alive and incredibly clear. My soul knew him. It had known him for a very long time, and it would want him for lifetimes more.

I reached for him. As I placed my arm against his chest, I felt his rock-like muscles against my palms. I didn't talk myself out of what happened next. I lifted my chin to his lips and kissed him, sealing our mating bond forever.

I'M HERE TO TAKE EVERYTHING
FROM THEM...

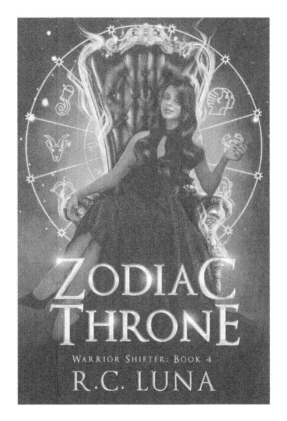

READ A SNEAK PEAK OF THE NEXT
BOOK IN THIS CAPTIVATING SERIES...

PREVIEW ZODIAC THRONE

CHAPTER 1

T he thousands of tiny suns at the very top of the massive Underworld cave dimmed as they faded off into the distance. A Zol orb glowed above me and the misty shape of the UnZol King, Balastar Ramon del Castillo.

Carly continued channeling the power of zodiac magic through the orb in order to bring the ancient UnZol King forth from the Void after the kiss that would forever make us Zol Mates. My hands, which had been shaking the entire climb up the side of the pyramid, stopped shaking the moment I made contact with the essence of my Zol Mate, the UnZol King. And all at once, everything felt right. At the moment that my lips grazed his phantom face, I was overwhelmed by a feeling of trust. Releasing myself to trust anyone was an impossibly hard thing to do; every tough lesson I'd had learned in my young adult life had taught me not to.

In the days leading up to the rite, Carly and I had spent a lot of time together. She told me how she had studied all the old scrolls and books about these ancient ceremonies to make sure her rite was executed with precision. She had spoken with awe when she'd described the time the death god Vucub-Cane had gone over all of it with her, taking the time to check her spells, her form and the timing of her movements.

"It is critical that you enter the rite with a truly open heart," Carly had said when she was preparing me for today. "It doesn't matter how the stars brought you here. What matters is that, when you're standing in front of him and make your first contact under the Zol orb, your heart is pure."

"How can my heart be pure when so much corruption has brought me to this point?" I'd asked. All I could think about before the rite was that everything about our mate bond was tainted and toxic.

To start off, the relics—which were created from the body parts of the UnZol King himself—had brought nothing but death and destruction to the worlds of Zol Stria and Earth. Then I got blamed for the destruction of Zol Stria because of a prophecy, got chased, captured and thrown in the Zodiac prison by the death god Hun-Cane. Then his twin brother and also death god Vucub-Cane kidnapped me and now I found myself in a beautiful black dress mating the Unzol King. These were all a series of unexpected chain of disasterous events that kept getting bigger and more elaborate as the days went on.

But Carly insisted that I could find a reason to actually want to mate the ghost king. In those days before she would say, "You must find a motivator that is true for you. Search your soul and find a genuine, honest reason why being mated to the UnZol King, and helping us bring him out of the Void and into this world, is something you want."

Many nights I considered rejecting him. I visualized myself standing up on that platform and refusing to go through with it all. Maybe I would shift into my jaguar form and make a run for it. Of course, Vucub-Cane would stop me in my tracks with his mind control, just like Hun-Cane did right before he threw me in prison. And this is all besides that fact that if f I rejected a Zol Mate, we would both be doomed to an eternity of unhappiness in love. It meant I would never find love again and that any relationships I would have would be ill-fated.

But I didn't care much about that. I wasn't going through with this mating bond to avoid a tragic love life. I had managed to have a tragic love life just fine all on my own. No. I was doing this because I didn't want my unit to be punished anymore. I didn't want anyone else I loved to die. And I was hoping that what I had learned about Balastar being a savior for the oppressed was true. Yet none of those reasons were the true motivator. Just beneath the surface, there was something even stronger than all those reasons, and it was what kept my heart pure at the moment that I swept my lips against his.

It must have been the right reason because after we made contact a charge tingled over my skin. My gossamer skirt swooshed as a cool breeze swept around us. Even with the watching eyes of thousands of spectators below, in that instant we were alone.

His kiss didn't linger. Instead, it was the briefest of kisses, but it was enough to commence the return of the UnZol King. In my head I had gotten used to calling him by his real name, Balastar. For whatever reason, it felt more natural that way.

Lights sparked around him, glimmering, and speckled, and they glowed brilliantly as they lit him up from the inside out like a captive star. My eyes grew wide as I watched magic cover him in a glowing sheen. I took a few steps back and tried to keep my mind from racing as it began to sink in that this was all really happening.

Would he fight for the freedom of all people, or just the Dark Zodiac? Would he help me get what I wanted most of all, which was to be free from the command of the death gods? I wanted all the nagual to live free, not as slaves subject to the whims of gods. Hope for our freedom was the motivator that had brought me to the top of the obsidian pyramid. I knew it would be complicated, perhaps it would even be an impossible task, but if anyone could help me fight for our freedom, it would be my Zol Mate.

As the UnZol King took a step back and blinked at me, the urge to trust him returned. I decided not to resist the feelings stirring for my mate, curious at the emotions that were starting to rise from within my Zol. I didn't expect to feel this happy that he was coming back. It was like I just couldn't wait to see him in the flesh again. It was like this was the greatest thing that could ever happen. It was like fireworks on New Year's and dancing to your favorite song. This feeling of happiness for someone I didn't even know, was strange in my logical brain but not in my body. For a moment, it felt too good to allow myself to worry about it. I let myself trust that everything would be ok, including this.

The unexpected happiness coursing through me began to mix with another feeling. Loneliness rushed to the surface. That was when I realized I had missed him. Deep in my reincarnated soul, I had missed him. A single tear fell from my eye, and my lips quivered in relief as though I had been waiting an eternity for this to happen. His phantom hand reached up and cradled my jaw, unsuccessfully wiping my tear with a shimmering ghost of a thumb.

"Balastar," I whispered. Zol knows why the combination of syllables that made up his name felt more familiar now than they ever had before.

He was still a mystery, and the more I explored the emotions coursing through me, the more I knew they weren't rational. They came from some place deep inside of me. It was a part of me I didn't yet understand.

He shifted his gaze around the platform, reaching his hands out in front of him and opening and closing them as though he hadn't done that in a long time. Then he shifted his blank, unreadable gaze to the Devil's Eye around my neck.

Carly stepped forward and stood between us. She took the Devil's Eye necklace in one hand and swept her other hand over it as she chanted in the ancient language of the Zol Sen. A stream of golden light shot from the Zol orb and the Eye crumbled to ash. Its ashes rose into a tiny, dark-energy tornado that crackled and hummed with power. She opened her palms and channeled the tornado at him. It headed directly for his eyes and funneled right into them. Soon after he became noticeably more of this world than that of the Void. His eyes revealed more depth than they had before, as though there was a Zol in there, somewhere. I looked down, and where the eye-shaped stone had been, now there was nothing except the silver frame that had held it in place.

Carly repeated the process with each of the relics, and with each one he became more alive and present than before. By the time she finished, there was no Blood Ruby on the ring I wore. When I looked at the table, the Obsidian

Heart was also gone, along with the Stone Mind and the Blade Bone. The Snake Tongue's sheath was wide open, but there was nothing inside. Every relic had disappeared.

The few Fae on the platform with us bowed before him, me included. I was overwhelmed with awe and my honor compelled me to acknowledge the wonder before me with the bow. Vucub-Cane was the only one who didn't lower his head at the King. Instead, the death god approached Balastar and met his gaze, eye to eye.

"Welcome back," he said simply, and Balastar nodded.

Vucub-Cane cocked his head, and I wondered what the god was thinking. Was that concern on his face?

"Darkness reborn, serve the Zol as one," Balastar said, his voice breaking as though it was a strain to say the words.

"Ah, yes. There you are." Vucub-Cane patted Balastar on the shoulder.

Carly concentrated on Balastar, chanting spells and casting protection wards on him. She had told me he would be at his most vulnerable upon his return, disoriented and confused. In order to stabilize him, she would work a number of spells, all intertwined, to speed up the acclimation of his Zol skin.

Vucub-Cane turned to the crowd with outstretched arms, and the crowd released cheers and hollers. In a voice as loud as thunder, he said to them, "Zol Stria, your god Vucub-Cane has answered your prayers. Today we bring you the Master Zol Sen with the power of a god, the one who is destined to give you your freedom." The death god motioned his right hand to where Balastar stood; his hooded eyes revealed nothing. The crowd hollered and cheered so loudly the trees in the surrounding black forest shook from the commotion.

"He will no longer linger in the merciless Void. This is the time for all of Zol Stria to unite as one. Humans and Fae will live together. The stars write the path." Vucub-Cane took several steps back, and Balastar moved forward.

Somewhere to my left, Carly muttered under her breath, "He still doesn't know where he is. He's been in the Void for far too long." She bit her lip as she studied him.

The crowd clapped and yelled as the UnZol King stood before them. He scanned the mass of Fae in attendance aimlessly, and finally, his blank look gave way to a pinched brow and slight grimace.

Knights of the UnZol Army stood in three long lines at the very front of the crowd. They were dressed in black battle gear with gray armor over the top and the symbol for the Underworld embossed in red over the right breast. As the crowd cheered behind them, they looked forward with concentrated, earnest expressions. They slowly lowered their swords to the side, dropped into a kneel and bowed upon seeing Balastar. The crowd began to quiet shortly after and, row by row, the attendees kneeled as the silence grew among them.

Their loyalty to him after all this time shocked me. It was true, then, that the chosen ones were never forgotten.

"How much longer do we have to be up here?" I whispered to Carly from the side of my mouth.

Her eyes darted to me, then to the death god. She approached Balastar and linked her arm with his. She turned to Vucub-Cane and said, "Your Grace, I must take him inside now to complete the process."

The death god nodded, and she proceeded to enter the enclosed stairs that led down into the pyramid. The crowd released a series of murmurs as he left the platform. I considered following after them—part of me wanted to be sure he was ok—but something kept my feet planted there on the platform, standing before the masses.

"The stars have written that your king shall have a warrior queen as a Zol Mate." Vucub-Cane gestured toward me and I stepped forward. "Fate brings you Queen Sasha. She has been tested and has passed every trial. Her heart is pure. She wants nothing more than to fight for freedom for you all."

Rumbling reverberated through the crowd. After a few heartbeats the faint sound of clapping could be heard, which I assumed was from my unit. The seconds that passed with only a series of low murmurs had me gritting my teeth as my chest tightened. Then the crowd's chattering evolved into a continuous stream of what sounded like courtesy claps. Carly had explained that much of this new generation had only heard legends of the UnZol King and not much about his queen. This made it hard for them to understand who she was, and for the Fae, respect had to be earned. It was never just given. I realized then that there was much to learn about this new role, but more than that, it seemed my work was cut out for me to win over this crowd.

As the murmurs died down, the death god said, "Now, let's celebrate the return of the UnZol King."

With those words, the crowd's cheers exploded.

I released a ragged breath, glad this part was over. Whatever else was coming would have to wait until I'd had at least a couple shots of tequila.

Read more in the...
Warrior Shifter Series

YOU READY FOR MORE?

I truly hoped you enjoyed this book. There's so much more to the universe of Zol Stria that I can't wait to tell you about. Join my newsletter to receive the prequel FREE, updates on my new books and the books of other amazing authors.

Visit this link to get it today: www.rcluna.com

And it would mean so much to me if you would leave a review on Amazon and GoodReads. Your reviews are so important. They help readers decide if this book is right for them. Please help me get the books I've worked so hard on in the hands of the right readers.

Keep reading for a preview of Zodiac Throne, the epic final book in the Warrior Shifter Series.

Truly grateful for you!
R.C. Luna

About the Author

R.C. Luna is a moon child who believes we are all made of stardust.

Her passion for books, magic, witchcraft and mystery comes alive with the sexy, paranormal monsters that line the pages of her books. Her characters are driven by the phases of the moon and the alignment of the stars.

Luna's experience as a Puerto Rican growing up in South Florida influences her writing of multicultural storylines, as does her time spent in the U.S. Air Force and living in several different Latin American countries.

Darkness is her playground, and you'll find her up well into the night reading fantasy romance novels.

Sign up for her newsletter and receive the FREE prequel – Zodiac Shadows, along with updates on the latest releases in her series, *Warrior Shifter* and free fantasy books from great authors on the regular.

www.rcluna.com

KEEP IN TOUCH

Let's keep in touch!
www.rcluna.com
TikTok @author_rcluna
Facebook @authorrcluna
Instagram @author_rcluna

Made in the USA
Coppell, TX
24 February 2025

46376818R00094